Unfinished Business

LaChaurie "L.A." Jefferson

L.A Jefferson

Detroit, Michigan

Cover design by Ubangi Graphics

Partial typesetting provided by HubBooks Literary Service

Please visit this author's website:

http://lajefferson.com

To contact this author, email at: charmie2420@yahoo.com

Dedication

To my family and friends

who supported along the way. I

couldn't have done this without you.

Thank You

First and foremost, I thank God for the gift He gave me and the power to keep pushing on and believing in my abilities. Next, to those who were always there for me as I inched toward this accomplishment, I'll never forget you. You know who you are. And finally, a BIG thank you to the readers

ONE

S o, Lydia. You never did explain to us why you broke up with Roy. I thought things were going so well between the two of you." Sandra, Lydia's best friend of well over twenty years was yelling over the music. The latest Reggae dance groove by Sean Paul was blaring from the speakers that were far too close to their table. Unfortunately, there weren't any other tables available. The Good Life Lounge, a popular tri-level dance club for the mature crowd in downtown Detroit, was living up to its Thursday night reputation as being the liveliest place to be after work. People were packed in like sardines on all floors. Lydia was so into the music, doing the chair-dancing thing that she noticed Sandra's lips moving, but didn't quite hear what she said.

"What?" Lydia asked, squinting her round brown eyes. After Sandra repeated her question, Lydia wished she still hadn't heard her. "I don't have to give you an explanation, Sandra." Lydia rolled her eyes. "All you really need to know is that we broke up."

"To say "we" insinuates a mutual breakup. The way *I* understand it is that you broke up with him," Sandra said pointedly, shifting her intense coffee brown eyes to their other friend Kania. "Did you know that Roy wanted to marry this fool? And what does she do? Dumps him."

Kania gasped, clearly not believing her ears. "You said no! I just knew he was the one. I mean, you haven't been involved with anyone that heavy since…"

Lydia held her right hand up, palm facing her two friends as if to say, *Don't go there.* "I thought we were here celebrating your good news, not discussing my love life," she directed to Kania, who gestured her concurrence.

The trio of women had been friends since high school, Lydia and Sandra even earlier than that. When they graduated high school, Lydia and Sandra weren't ready to separate from each other so they attended Michigan State University together. But the ever-independent Kania was bold and brave enough to venture off to Atlanta, Georgia where she didn't know a soul.

Once they were all back in Detroit, they tried to get together at least twice a month for a little girlfriend bonding. But it didn't always work out that way. Instead, they managed a consistent once a month get-together. Lydia was the wannabe gourmet chef of the three and she would sometimes dazzle them with her culinary skills with homemade meals at her place. Other times, they'd meet at Sandra's for some kind of carryout meal and game night, or for drinks at different venues around the city.

It wasn't often they did the nightclub thing, but this month, Kania was in a partying mood. There were a couple of things she was celebrating.

Shortly after they arrived at the club, and were seated with their drinks, Kania announced that she'd been promoted to junior partner at the law firm she'd been working at for the past two years. While they were thrilled over that news, Kania followed that announcement with an even more exciting one. She and her longtime boyfriend, Kenneth, had just become engaged! The ladies screamed in unison, drawing many inquisitive stares their way.

Kania and Kenneth had been dating since they met in law school in his hometown of Atlanta, Georgia. When they graduated, they weren't all that sure what was going to happen with their relationship and they agreed not to let their relationship interfere with their careers. So they both ended up accepting positions in their own hometowns, Kania in Detroit and Kenneth in Georgia. If they were meant to be together, they figured it would just end up that way. They were right. The distance between them was instrumental in leading them to the decision of making the ultimate commitment to each other. Although they'd been talking about getting married over the past few months, Kania swore she was still blown away when Kenneth proposed on his last visit to Detroit a couple weeks ago.

It was still up in the air where Kania and Kenneth would settle. Both of them graduated at the top of their law classes and were currently working for very reputable law firms. Neither would have any problem getting a job. The idea of starting a husband/wife practice wasn't a far off idea either. Right now, making plans to become husband and wife was their primary focus.

Kania was trying to play her usual cool role, but Lydia could see the happiness and excitement plastered across her face. A few times she glanced across the table and caught a wide grin on Kania's face. But Kania would point out something happening on the dance floor or something elsewhere in the club as though that was what she was laughing at. Lydia couldn't help but laugh. Kania was just being Kania, always calm, cool, and collected. That was Kania—yesterday, today, and forever.

They were at the club for about three hours. After far too many dances with way too many wannabe pimps and playas, who weren't worth the played out pickup lines that slithered from their lips and another round of drinks, the three of them were ready to call it a night. They had a ball, just like any other time they hung out and promised to do it again in a few weeks.

After hugging her girlfriends and sharing more congratulatory hugs and kisses, Kania climbed into her emerald green Pontiac G-6, which the valet attendant had pulled around only seconds before. "I'll call you guys in a few weeks with more details for the wedding," she called out before peeling away from the front of the club.

A few cars later, Lydia was dragging herself into the passenger side of Sandra's midnight black Lexus. She opened her eyes just enough to see the clock on the dashboard. Two-thirty. God, she was surely going to regret the fun she had tonight when her alarm clock in a few short hours.

This was definitely the wrong night for Lydia to be hanging out like wet clothes. Tomorrow she was to do a very important presentation for the senior management team of the IT Division to present her proposal for the company's marketing effort for their large business accounts.

Global-Tel had hired Lydia right after college graduation to an entry-level management position as an administrative assistant in the Consumer Division. Two years later, which was in alignment with her five-year career plan, Lydia was promoted to a supervisory position in Sales & Service. Now she was vying, along with two of her peers, Angela Robinson and Stanley DuVall, for an upcoming senior management position. Angela Robinson was a middle-aged Black woman, with over thirty years of service with the company. Most were wondering why in the heck she waited so late to try advancing her career. Stanley DuVall, on the other hand, was a White forty-something man, former union board member attempting to use his chumminess with management to move up. The current senior manager, Roger Daniels, would be retiring in about six months. But as soon as she heard about the upcoming vacancy, Lydia already claimed it as hers.

"You were wrong as hell to bring Roy up like that," Lydia charged as soon as Sandra pulled onto the street. Ever since Sandra made her comments in the club, Lydia couldn't wait to plunge into her the minute they were alone. She had only held her tongue earlier so she and Sandra wouldn't argue while they were celebrating Kania's good news.

Nonchalantly, Sandra replied. "I just asked you a question. Maybe if you didn't feel guilty, you wouldn't be so bothered."

The throbbing in her temple almost kept Lydia from lifting her head off the headrest, but she managed anyway. "Look Sandra, you were out of line bringing that up tonight, or any night for that matter. You seem to be the only person who doesn't respect the decisions I make regarding my personal life. Maybe if you spent half as much time keeping track of that cheating ass husband of yours, you wouldn't be in your current predicament." As angry as she was, Lydia still knew she'd gone too far with her last words. She had hit way below the belt.

"Fuck you!" Sandra snapped, while abruptly forcing her gear into park after she pulled into Lydia's driveway. "You don't know shit. I have a family and there is more to consider than just *my* own feelings." Sandra paused to take a breath. "If you haven't noticed, Lydia, you're not getting any younger. Even as independent as Kania is, she's smart enough to know what to do when you have a good man who's ready to commit to you.

"Not you, though. You just push the good ones like Roy away. Ohhh," she continued dramatically, "but let ole no good ass Thomas show back up on the scene and you become a merciful little puppy at his feet."

Lydia cut her eyes sharply in Sandra's direction. Without uttering another word, she angrily pushed open the door and walked into her house.

TWO

Preparing for work the next morning, Lydia was still steaming over the highly tempered exchange she and Sandra had the night before. The aromatherapy shower did absolutely nothing to calm her. Nor did drinking a cup of her favorite Belgian Chocolate Nut coffee.

Sitting at her kitchen table, Lydia shook her head pitifully. It was pointless trying to stay angry with Sandra for sticking her nose in her business. What else was new? Sandra had been doing that since they became friends over twenty years ago. Throughout their school years together, and beyond, Sandra was always finding ways to instigate in various aspects of Lydia's life, especially her love life.

Sandra had never been able to accept that although she and Lydia were as close as two friends could be, their personalities were like day and night. Sandra was all about image, money, and prestige. She craved the appearance of having more than the next person. During her dating years, no matter how nice and sweet a man was to Sandra, if he didn't have deep pockets and a free hand with his money, Sandra dropped him like a hot potato.

Lydia, on the other hand, didn't want to pay the price she usually associated with men who gave too freely. She knew most men believed that if they were spending their cash on you, then you'd better be giving something back in return. Oh sure, they might play the role like they were just that into you. But Lydia eventually felt that a man like that would have a woman right where he wanted her—under his control. Lydia refused to be controlled by anyone.

Lydia felt that the most important thing about a man she was involved with was his personality. He had to have a good head on his shoulders and be about taking care of his business. In a word—responsible. It wasn't all about what kind of job the brotha had, as long as he had a decent one.

How Lydia vibed with a man's spirit was also important. When she was in a relationship, she didn't like things feeling as if they were forced. She felt that things should fall right into place if they were meant to be. She looked for her heart to palpitate at the very thought of her man, not of how much money he would spend on her. Although she wouldn't be mad at some spending.

Lydia and Sandra were the best of friends, but they couldn't be more different. They grew up in the same neighborhood, attended the same schools and had many of the same friends. But that's where the similarities ended.

The only real father figure Sandra had ever known, literally, took the first plane out of her life when he discovered that Sandra wasn't his biological daughter when Sandra was only five years old. After that, the only consistency Sandra knew of a male figure was that there would always be one around. Sandra's mother, Stephanie, had a man for every reason a woman could think of. One to help with household bills, one for car repairs, another one for house repairs, and a few in between to keep her mother's pockets lined with money. Everyone, including Sandra, speculated what Stephanie did in return for the men in her life.

Only Stephanie knew for sure. Thankfully, Sandra didn't follow totally in her mother's footsteps. While Sandra didn't require several men to take of her needs, she did believe in having that ONE to take care of them all.

Lydia's situation was completely different. Her parents were married, seemingly happy for most of her adolescent years. Then, one day, her father didn't come home from work. The days turned into weeks.

The weeks into months. Eventually her mother, Caroline, received divorce papers in the mail. There was no point in fighting for a marriage the man obviously didn't want to be in anymore, so Caroline signed the papers and shipped them off. After the divorce, Caroline had to redefine her priorities. She was already working part-time at a hotel in reservations. But, having become suddenly single, and the head of the household, she had to focus on bringing enough money into the house to maintain the comfortable lifestyle that she and Lydia had become accustomed to. So she began working full-time at the hotel and taking college courses part-time towards a degree in hospitality management. Not wanting her daughter to have that same struggle, Caroline made it clear to Lydia that she must advance her education and be career-focused so that she would never have to be financially dependent on any man.

Although Sandra knew Lydia, almost better than her own mother, when she played matchmaker, the men she chose usually met her own credentials rather than Lydia's, which drove Lydia nuts. Most of the men looked to be straight off the cover of GQ Magazine, with attitudes and personalities to match. Like they were God's gift to women. Lydia barely made it through the dates without her stomach turning several times at some of the shallow things that came out of their mouths.

Considering their history of Sandra's unsuccessful matchmaking, it was no wonder that Lydia's first response was a heartfelt "NO" when Sandra swore she had the perfect guy for Lydia two years ago. Sandra begged and pleaded for an entire week, promising that Lydia wouldn't be disappointed.

Due to a combination of a dating drought and being tired of Sandra's relentless pestering, Lydia finally agreed to go out with the mystery man on a double date with Sandra and her husband, Lester. She nearly doubled over with laughter when the mystery man turned out to be Roy Collins! Lydia and Roy, Sandra's cousin, had met and become close friends over ten years before.

Lydia had met Roy on one of Sandra's family reunion outings to Cedar Pointe Amusement Park in Sandusky, Ohio. She was a senior in high school, Roy was in his second year in college at Georgia State University. Roy didn't bother trying to hide his attraction to Lydia. He went on and on about how cute Lydia was and how he couldn't believe that she didn't have, nor had ever had, a boyfriend.

"You must be one of those psycho girls behind that pretty face," he joked, putting on a very convincing perplexed expression on his face.

Lydia liked Roy immediately. Not only was he cute, he was sweet, with an easygoing way about himself.

Most importantly, he kept her laughing! Lydia's mother was very tough on her about keeping her grades up and participating in extracurricular activities so she could get a full scholarship to college that there wasn't much time for serious dating. Her aloof demeanor, coupled with her pretty face and athletic, but feminine, figure only made the boys want her more. But knowing her mother wasn't one to play with, most of the boys contented themselves with being her friend.

So except for dates to school dances and occasional dates to the movies, Lydia never had the opportunity to get serious with anyone in high school. That made the time she spent with Roy on the Cedar Pointe trip even more special. They connected in a way she never experienced. She had never had as much fun with anyone, other than her girlfriends. Roy even managed to help her tackle her fear of roller coasters. Having him to hold on to was enough to suppress her fear and have loads of fun!

Before they departed, Lydia and Roy exchanged phone numbers and addresses, and agreed to stay in touch. For months, they were steady with letters, phone calls, and eventually emails. Then, Lydia became wrapped up in the exciting activities of her senior year, like homecoming activities, dances, and the senior picnic. Roy, too, became heavily involved in his college studies and activities. So, before the year passed, their long distance relationship dwindled to sporadic communication through Sandra, but they both still considered themselves good friends.

Two years passed before they saw each other again. Again, it was at another one of Sandra's family functions. It was obvious that there was still an attraction between them. At the time, though, Lydia had fallen in love with Thomas Cunningham and Roy was involved with someone, too.

The next time around when Sandra set them up on a blind date, neither of them was involved with anyone else. The timing couldn't have been better. Exploring a relationship with each other was something they'd both always wanted to do, and in no time their relationship blossomed. Since the first time they met, and even over the years that they had been involved with other people, the attraction and underlying feelings between them were alive and well.

In the beginning of their newfound relationship, they could barely keep their hands off each other—probably because it was something they'd always longed to do. But, when they were actually about to make love for the first time, Roy surprisingly put on the brakes, knocking Lydia completely off guard.

Roy told Lydia that he wanted something more from her than he'd had with other women. He said that he was tired of having great sex in relationships, but nothing of significance outside of the bedroom. He wanted his and Lydia's relationship to have substance, something lasting.

They spent the next six months of their relationship engaging in endless foreplay while learning the ins and outs of each other's lives. They would talk for hours, about a long range of subjects. They had fun enjoying the different activities each other liked—inline skating, biking, bowling, and going to the movies.

Their love for each other grew to an intensity Lydia never experienced with anyone. Lydia was not used to this new kind of love she was experiencing with Roy. She had only known the love of one man, Thomas Cunningham. The love she shared with him was vastly different from what she shared with Roy. With Thomas things had always been dangerously passionate, addictive. Lydia broke all of her rules, doing things she never imagined of herself.

Roy wasn't the kind of man to make a woman break her rules. He loved Lydia for the woman she was, not for who he wanted her to be. And Lydia loved him, just as he was—a sweet, kind, gentle, loving man. Plus, he was the only man that she'd been able to love besides Thomas. For that alone, he had to be special.

Lydia was comfortable with her and Roy's relationship. Then Roy wanted to change that. He wanted more. Marriage. For her own reasons, Lydia couldn't let that happen. Undoubtedly, she loved Roy. In fact, she had even imagined them getting married someday. But she knew she needed to complete some unfinished business from her past before that could happen.

It was pointless trying to make everybody—Roy, her mother, and her friends—understand her hesitation. It didn't even make sense to her.

How could she make anyone understand how after all she'd been through with Thomas Cunningham—after all he'd done to her, after he hurt and embarrassed her—why she had allowed him back into her life? While her good senses told her to run as fast as she could in the opposite direction when she caught sight of Thomas approaching her three weeks ago, the passion-filled memories she'd never been able to shake off got the better of her.

THREE

It was the week after Lydia had returned to work from a two-week vacation. She and her mother had enjoyed five glorious days on one of the newest Royal Caribbean cruise line ships, *The Enchantment*. It was Royal's most elegant cruise liner. Neither of them had been on a cruise before, so simply setting foot on the largest all-inclusive entertainment structures either of them had ever seen had them awe struck from beginning to end. Talk about endless fun and excitement. Neither of them were gamblers, yet they hit the slot machines in the casinos every night. Daringly, Lydia even took a chance on the blackjack table a few times, and won, too! Docking on the islands was just a relaxing break from the fun they were having on the ship.

The week after that, Lydia simply relaxed at home and did a little cleaning and much needed, reorganizing. When she dragged herself back to work, she had a ton of work to catch up on. Luckily, with the exception of a few people coming into her office to inquire about her vacation, scan through the pictures they threatened her not to forget at home, and pick up the souvenir necklaces she brought for them, there weren't too many distractions to keep her from her work. Still, Lydia put in long hours to get things caught up by the end of the week. She arrived at work by seven in the morning. And it was well after seven in the evening when she was heading home.

Lydia couldn't help but notice that every day she stayed late, so did Angela and Stanley, Lydia's two competitors for the senior management position. She was sure there was no other reason for this besides ensuring that Lydia, alone, didn't stand out for her dedication to work. When she was leaving work on this particular day, Stanley was walking over to the parking structure located one block over from the building. Since she come in so early that morning, she'd been lucky enough to get a space in the front of the parking structure.

"Thank God," she thought as they reached the entrance of the parking structure. She and Stanley made all the small talk they possibly could have made in the short walk. The sight of her midnight blue Jeep Grand Cherokee was the best vision Lydia had had all day. Lydia waved a professionally mandated farewell to Stanley before opening the rear door to place her Coach carrying case behind her seat.

An eerie feeling suddenly came over Lydia as soon as Stanley was out of sight. One of those creepy feelings you get when you're at home by yourself in the wee hours of the morning and you hear a scary sound that you know better than to get up and investigate. As she and Stanley had walked across the street, Lydia thought she had caught the eye of someone watching them from a light brown Ford Taurus parked at one of the meters towards the end of the block. But when she turned toward the driver, they pulled off. Now as she was securing herself in her seatbelt, from the rearview mirror, it looked like the same brown Taurus was parked three cars over from her. She wanted to believe that the car belonged to an employee or to someone picking up an employee. But her gut was just telling her otherwise. Lydia was a smart woman. She knew not to ignore that gut, so she didn't waste any more time getting the hell out of that lot! Maybe it was paranoia from the long hours she'd been working. Then, maybe not. Either way, she felt a heck of a lot better once she was on I-96 heading toward home.

The good feeling of relief didn't last very long, though. A few exits before the one she took to get to her house, she saw that the same Taurus was two cars behind her in the next lane. Lydia panicked and immediately reached for her cell phone, which for some God-awful reason was dead. She'd been so tired the last few nights, that she hadn't thought to re-charge her phone. *Damn!*

Finally, the safety tips that often came through her email from friends paid off. Lydia knew not to go home. Instead, she took the next exit that came up and looked for the nearest gas station. Her mind was racing far too fast to remember where the nearest police station was.

She saw a Mobile gas station two traffic lights after she exited the freeway. She pulled into the entrance. And that *damn* Taurus pulled right in behind her. *These crazy people have no shame,* Lydia thought to herself. All in one motion, Lydia was unbuckling her seatbelt and opening her door to hurry inside when a man's all-too-familiar voice called out her name.

"Lydia."

Suddenly, it was as if time had stopped. She felt suspended in her steps, hardly able to turn around But she did. He called out to her again.

"Lydia. I'm sorry if I scared you." She couldn't believe she was looking at Thomas Cunningham, the finest, sexiest, most sexually satisfying man she'd dated. He'd captured, and then broke her heart. Yet, she found him irresistible. But, still, he scared the shit out of her!

Finally, her voice surfaced to her throat, and then out of her mouth. "Thomas, what the hell are you doing here?" Before he opened his mouth, both of them already knew the answer to that. It was the same unspoken reason he always had for abruptly reappearing in her life whenever he felt inclined to do so. To reclaim what he had always believed to be his—Lydia.

The last time Thomas deserted her was three years ago, leaving her to look like a fool in the eyes of her loved ones, and she vowed that would be the last time. Oh, she knew he'd be back again. Like her mother always said, "A leopard never changes his spots." After she had picked up the pieces of her shattered heart, Lydia vowed to do things differently when he came back the next time.

But now that that time seemed to have arrived, as he stood before her eyes, in his flawless, beautiful dark chocolate flesh, the strength she was so confident that she'd have wasn't there. Lydia felt weak, like a melting piece of hot wax, and she prayed it wasn't written all over her face. As he stepped all-knowingly toward her, he spoke in that delicious baritone voice that made her knees buckle.

"I'm back, baby," he began reaching his hand out to hers. "This time I'm back for good."

"For good," Lydia repeated, barely audible, she was so taken aback by the strength of his presence. It disgusted her. "And what does that have to do with me?" she asked, with a mock courageousness they both knew had been rehearsed.

"How about I tell you over a drink?" Thomas asked, seductively gazing at her with those deep brown eyes she remembered getting lost in.

FOUR

—�֍—

The entrance lobby of Global-Tel was practically empty when Lydia walked through its double doors. Usually, it was filled with a bunch of employees huddled together in clusters, catching up on the latest office gossip, trying to hold out to the absolute last second before they had to sign on for the day's work. Surely a sign that the visiting higher-ups had arrived.

It was a quarter to nine, and Lydia had just under ten minutes to get to her office to do a quick run over of her presentation. She was a nervous wreck, knowing she should have allowed herself much more prep time, considering the significance of her task. Unfortunately, she suffered from an advance case of procrastinationitis. Rushing past a peer or two and a handful of her employees, she chirped a quick "good morning," and received a few "good lucks."

Her boss and mentor, Marianne Spalding, was waiting inside her office when Lydia walked in. Lydia wasn't totally surprised. Marianne was a spunky black woman who'd started her career with Global-Tel, back in the mid-seventies, when the company had a monopoly over the telecommunications industry. Like a lot of the managers with her years of seniority, Marianne had spent many years as a non-management, union represented employee in various craft jobs. Then, by being in the right relationship with the right people, she was selected to participate in a management trainee program, which eventually led to a promotion to an entry-level management position. She'd spent the last ten years building on those relationships and creating new ones, into which she'd brought Lydia as well.

In a way, Lydia's success or failure with the presentation would be a reflection on Marianne, as Lydia had been her protégé since she was hired into the company fulltime. Needless to say, Marianne was as nervous as Lydia.

"Wow, you're cutting it down to the wire, aren't you?" Marianne asked. Marianne sat cross-legged in the chair in front of Lydia's desk, a beautiful pair of diamond teardrop earrings dangling from her ears. "My girl must already have this thing hemmed up tight, huh?"

Lydia smiled at Marianne's obvious sarcasm. "Hey, you know some of us just have it like that," she returned with clearly over-indulged confidence.

"Alright, seriously. You ready? That must be what this arriving just in the nick of time business is all about." Marianne's tone was calm, but through squinted sharp eyes she added, "You better not screw this up, girlfriend."

"I'm feeling pretty confident. I just need a few minutes to look over my notes, and I'll be ready," Lydia offered.

Marianne stood to leave, smoothing down the front of the ivory knee length straight skirt she was wearing. "It's no secret I've got great confidence in you. I know you'll be great. See you in the conference room in a few."

When Marianne was gone, Lydia kept to her word and skimmed over her notes. This presentation was probably one of the most important deciding factors for who would be promoted into the senior manager position. Over the last couple of weeks, Angela and Stanley had already been put to the test with their presentations. From what she had heard, neither of them sucked. So Lydia couldn't afford to screw up. She needed perfection. After reciting a quick prayer, Lydia gathered up her note cards and headed to the conference room.

Two hours later, Marianne was treating Lydia to a celebratory lunch at Sweet Georgia Brown, a popular upscale restaurant, which featured live Jazz music located downtown Detroit on the corner of Brush Street.

"You know you're my girl, right!" Marianne chimed, excitedly. "The way you shined during that presentation, I'd rank you above my own daughter," she teased, grinning. They clinked their glasses of sparkling Sprite—they weren't off the clock yet.

"Okay, now, you know Denise is my friend. I just might have to use that statement as leverage against you to make sure I get this promotion," Lydia joked. She knew Marianne was just joking about liking her better than Denise. One of the many reasons Lydia and Marianne took so much to each other was that Marianne and Denise had the same close mother-daughter relationship that Lydia and her mother shared.

After several months of hearing about each other and how they were sure to get along, Lydia and Denise had finally met at Global-Tel's annual Christmas party a couple of years ago. They were close in age and had similar interests. Both were fitness fanatics. Lydia had played volleyball and ran track in high school and college. She exercised faithfully, rather than participating in organized sports. But Denise had Lydia beat. Denise loved fitness so much that she left a prestigious job in the banking industry to become a full-time personal trainer, and then eventually opened up her own fitness center.

Lydia was in awe at the grand opening of Fit Forever. Denise was the first person she'd known personally who actually had gone past the point of dreaming about what she wanted, to making it happen.

Immediately, Lydia dropped her membership at a more popular and larger fitness chain for the personal touch of Fit Forever, not to mention, for friendship. She even convinced Sandra, Kania, and a several Global-Tel employees to join too. At least twice a week, when Denise could manage to take some time from her personal training and managerial duties, she and Lydia hooked up for a rigorous game of racquetball.

"Oh, speaking of Denise," Marianne began just as the waiter arrived with their Cajun shrimp and grilled vegetables, "she's got a new cell phone number that she told me to give you, but it's in my office. Remind me when we get back."

"Don't worry about it. I'm supposed to see her at the gym after work when I go preview this new kickboxing instructor she's trying out," Lydia said.

Exasperation crossed Marianne's face. "My goodness! Haven't you been to that gym like three times already this week?" She took another swallow of her drink. "You and Denise's skinny behinds are prime examples of why I don't take my chunky self to anybody's gym. The only ones there are the people already in shape. If I ever want to work out, I'll do it in the privacy of my own bedroom, whenever I'm ready to clear the clothes off my treadmill."

They both laughed. Once they settled back down, Marianne resumed talking about what a great impression Lydia had made on the VP's. By the time they were on the way back to the office, Marianne had Lydia feeling like she had the senior management position in the bag!

Lydia was still on cloud nine when she left work. She had plenty of energy for the gym, where she was headed to now. When she arrived at Fit Forever, she was glad to see that the parking lot was not on jam yet. In about twenty minutes, the five o'clock crowd would be swarming the lot. Quickly, Lydia gathered her gym bag and headed inside.

For a change, Denise's was the first face she saw. Usually, Denise was in the back office dealing with the paperwork or phone calls.

"Hey, girl!" Denise shrieked, excitedly. She was comfortably dressed in a hot pink racer-back Reebok half tank, exposing the perfectly defined abs that Lydia was still working towards in black, loose-fitting sweatpants. "You know I thought you were going to forget, right?"

"That's precisely why I made a point to make it," Lydia teased, lacing her arm through Denise's. They hadn't gone three steps before they heard a voice from behind them.

"I didn't forget either." It was Sandra.

Lydia knew why Sandra was there. Still she asked, "What are you doing here?" Sandra was there for them to make amends for the argument they'd had the other night. It's funny, Lydia thought, how things between friends never change. Even when they were kids, whenever they got into it over something, serious or not, one of them would initiate the makeup within forty-eight hours. It had become an unspoken rule. It was also unspoken which one of them would do the apologizing. No wonder they were best friends.

Sandra wasn't an exercise enthusiast like Lydia and Denise. But every now and then, for bonding purposes, and to get a break from home, she would tag along to the gym with Lydia. She was fine, as long as she didn't break a sweat.

"Whoa, Sandra! You're going to do the kickboxing class too?" Denise asked, obviously shocked.

"I'll do it until it becomes too much. But I figured it'd be good to work off the apple pie I've been eating all afternoon," Sandra explained as Denise walked them to the ladies' locker room.

Hmmm, thought Lydia, Sandra eating apple pie meant only one thing. She and her husband, Lester, were having some serious problems. When troubles were brewing with Lester, which were more often than not, Sandra always turned to her favorite junk food, apple pie. It was a good thing Sandra had a naturally high metabolism or else she'd need to visit the gym much more frequently.

The instructor of the kickboxing class, Gregory Lytle was awesome. He reminded Lydia a little of that famous Black Tae Bo exercise instructor, Billy Blanks, only he was much more attractive. Forty-five minutes of strenuous side and front kicking and jabbing fully drained all fifteen participants in the class, judging from the sluggishness with which everyone dragged themselves out of the door. All except Sandra, who took breaks every five to seven minutes.

"You don't even have to ask if I'll be doing that class again. I had to take far too many breaks to make it through that class," Sandra said as she and Lydia headed towards the locker room.

Lydia laughed in response. "How 'bout we relax in the sauna for awhile? Do you have some time?"

"Sure." Sandra answered.

Expectedly, the sauna room was empty. Not many people came to the gym on Friday nights. Most were too busy trying to go hang out in the streets or cozying up with their significant others. Lydia knew full-well about that. Until a couple of months ago, that's what she had been doing with Roy.

She and Sandra had been in the sauna for about fifteen minutes, in a comfortable silence, before Sandra blurted out, "I was wrong as hell for bringing up you and Roy the other night the way I did. Not only was it the wrong time, but it was none of my business."

Wow! *None of her business.* Never in their entire friendship had Sandra admitted that something was none of her business. She was normally oblivious to that fact. Lydia guessed the saying was true, "There's a first time for everything."

"I'm sorry," Sandra added. They were lying on separate benches, allowing the hot steam in the sauna to open up their pores and relax their sore muscles.

Sincerely, Lydia returned, "It's okay, girl. I know I crossed the line with some things I said, too. I guess we were both minding a little too much of each other's business."

"Yeah, but you were more right about me than I was about you. Maybe it is something that I'm doing or not doing that keeps driving Lester to other women," Sandra said, surprising Lydia.

Lydia couldn't hide her appall. "Sandra, don't be crazy! Any woman with half a brain knows that a man cheats even when he has the best, most beautiful woman by his side. Halle Berry? Need I say more?" she exclaimed of Hollywood's noted most beautiful woman in America, who'd recently split from her self-professed sex addicted husband. "I could name some more notables, but I think my point is proven. So, don't even go there."

Their conversation was interrupted by the entrance of another woman. *"Damn,"* Lydia and Sandra mouthed silently towards each other. Cheating men may have been a universal topic amongst women, but neither of them was going to discuss Sandra's marital issues in front of a total stranger.

Strangely enough, though, the woman came in quite chatty. Apparently she had been in the kickboxing class with them.

"Oooh, girl!" the woman cooed, more to Lydia than Sandra, as she made room for herself on the bench Lydia was on. "You were really gettin' into that class. If you had been closer to the front of the class, I would've thought you were the teacher." Disbelievingly, the woman asked, "This wasn't your first class, was it?"

Not really sure how to respond to the woman's intense and sudden inquisitiveness, Lydia answered flatly. "I've been in other kickboxing classes before, but none as strenuous as this one."

"I thought it was pretty good, too," Sandra interjected. But the woman continued talking to Lydia as though Sandra hadn't uttered a word.

"Do you take other classes here?" The woman continued probing as she settled onto her spot on the bench.

"Yes. My friend, here," Lydia said alluding to Sandra, "and I take a few classes here during the week."

The woman continued pressing. "What days are you here? I know I'm coming off as pretty nosy, but I just joined this gym. And it'd be nice to work out with a familiar face." *Not faces*, again ignoring Sandra's presence. Sandra didn't seem the least bit concerned about it.

Lydia certainly wasn't about to give out her gym schedule! She didn't know this woman from Eve. But she didn't want to come off as rude. Rather than her desired response, "DON'T WORRY ABOUT IT!" she lied. "I don't really have a regular schedule. You know, I pretty much drop in whenever my schedule allows it."

Finally, Sandra opened her eyes enough to receive the "let's get out of here" signal that Lydia had been trying to slyly give her for the last few minutes. "I'll see you around, though. Okay?" Lydia said before she and Sandra quickly scooted their way out.

After showering and dressing, they were standing at the rear of Lydia's truck. Lydia was placing her gym bag in the trunk. "I know it wasn't just me. Was that not the strangest thing *ever*? I've never had a *woman* try to get at me like that. That was almost scary."

"Almost," Sandra repeated heavy with sarcasm as she dropped her own bag in the trunk of her car parked in the space next to Lydia's. "You sure you didn't dump my cousin to start a lesbian fling and this was your way of introducing her to me?" Sandra questioned, smiling.

"Yeah right. This definitely goes down in my book of kooky experiences," Lydia said as they both entered their vehicles. "Trust me. I'll be watching out for that one."

FIVE

*Y*ou've got mail," the animated, robotic voice greeted Lydia as she logged onto the AOL website from her home computer when she got in from the gym. She was pooped from the class, but knew it was best to check her e-mail now because tomorrow she'd have no chance after picking up her goddaughter, Alicia, Sandra's six-year-old daughter. Entertaining and keeping up with Alicia would be all Lydia would have time for. Literally.

Scrolling through her inbox, Lydia frowned at the host of junk mail, online newsletters that she'd regrettably signed up for, and retailers advertising the "best sale ever," and so on. Finally, she came across what she'd been subconsciously expecting. It was an email from Thomas.

Hey Lovely,

How long you gonna keep ignoring my emails? You

must not remember how persistent I am when it comes to going after what I want. And I want you. No games. No more disappearing acts. This is the real deal. Stop running, girl. I'm done hurting you. Just one more chance…

Thomas

One more chance? Ha! How he even managed to form the thought in his head was beyond the scope of her comprehension. Ever since she'd taken him up on his offer for drinks after he followed her to the gas station, Thomas had been bombarding Lydia with emails. That was the only contact she would allow.

That night, Lydia didn't talk much. Instead, she nibbled on barbeque wings and French fries, while Thomas did most of the talking. He began carefully with a long, overdue apology for the last disappearing act he pulled three years ago, which had brought them to their third go-round. He explained how he had been immediately ordered back to the military base in Texas where he was stationed at that time, and there was no time for him to call. From there, he had received orders to depart to Cuba for a twelve-month tour of duty. He claimed that he wrote her a letter explaining everything, but didn't realize until months later that he never mailed it. By then he knew how it looked, considering their past, and could only imagine what Lydia was thinking. Then he claimed that he has been too scared to contact her.

Not only was the apology and explanation coming about three years too late, there was no amount of apology that would make up for the embarrassment and humiliation she suffered because of him. The only thing of significance that she managed to say to him was that she needed some time to process everything.

When he audaciously asked her why, Lydia coolly responded, with a slight edge in her tone, "I think that goes without saying." They had said goodnight at the gas station, with an awkward hug. Thomas had promised to give Lydia her space, but he must've only meant it in the physical sense, because the emails started the very next day.

Thomas was full of shit, she knew, but she admired his nerve to step to her with it. Either he was one confident ass man, or Lydia had been one stupid ass woman for far too long for him to think he could just walk back into her life and pick up where they left off, which wasn't that great a place. With the track record Thomas had established, it would take a hundred times more than a couple of drinks, some wings, and a sexy ass smile to get one foot back into the door of Lydia's life. And this time, they'd be playing the game they started so long ago by a different set of rules—hers.

Their "game" began at a college campus party at the school she attended with Sandra and about thirty percent of her high school graduating class. At that particular time Lydia had completely buried herself in her schoolwork. She had done enough partying her freshmen and sophomore years in school and was ready to really focus on her future. Sandra, and many of their other friends, on the other hand, were always ready for a party.

The weekend after finals, everyone, except Lydia, was in a celebratory mood. Sandra refused to let Lydia stay cooped up in her room while everyone else was having fun, especially without any excuses of studying.

"Girl, it's time for you to let loose and have some fun for a change," Sandra encouraged, as she finished dressing herself in a fitted, hot pink, off the shoulder mini-dress. "You studied enough this past week to have aced your finals *and* mine, too. Tonight we're going to have some fun," she concluded, pulling Lydia off the sofa sleeper with one hand. Lydia decided that maybe Sandra was right, that she was due a little fun, and Lydia agreed to go as long as Sandra agreed not to criticize her for what she decided to wear. Lydia's taste was never jazzy enough for Sandra's.

Admittedly, the party was definitely off the hook. But Lydia just couldn't get into it. Her body felt like dancing along with all of her friends, but her mind restrained her. What she wanted, instead, more than anything, was to snuggle up under her comforter after a long, hot shower. After an hour and a half of turning down men left and right, Lydia told Sandra she was bailing. Sandra was having too much fun to try to talk her out of it.

As she began making her exit, she felt a slight, gentle tug at her arm. "I know the sexiest lady in the room is not trying to get out of here without dancing with even one brotha?"

Startled by the voice behind her, Lydia immediately turned around. When she did, she was instantly breath taken at the sight of his rugged good looks. He looked like the kind of guy her mother would've warned her to stay away from because he was just the type that she wouldn't be able to resist, and wasn't able to resist.

He stood before her, taking in every inch of her, causing beads of sweat to instantly form under her arm. For the first time in her life, Lydia experienced being undressed with a man's eyes. Shamefully, she enjoyed it, as she allowed him to guide her to the dance floor.

An attraction formed instantly between them. Lydia was in a hypnotic-like state on the dance floor under the strong, steady gaze of Thomas' eyes. Their eyes locked as they matched the swaying of each other's hips to the rhythmic sound of the music. Thomas' hands were all over her, including her breasts and butt, and Lydia liked it.

She did things on the dance floor with Thomas that she hadn't even done behind closed doors. Things she would have looked down on other girls for doing. But that's how everything was for her with Thomas—out of the ordinary yet filled with wild excitement.

Lydia was so turned on by Thomas that night, it was inevitable that they were destined to eventually engage in some exciting, hot, passionate sex. She had no idea, however, that it would happen that very night. When she entered Thomas's dorm room behind him slowly, nevertheless anxiously, he said gently and sensually, "You don't have to be afraid, Lydia. I'm who you've been saving it for."

How he knew that she was a virgin was beyond her, but she was so far gone by that point, his words were the last thing on her mind. He placed soft, wet kisses on her neck and behind her ears, and in the cleavage of her firm breasts. Lydia melted upon impact.

All of the fears of sex that her mother implanted in her head while she was growing up vanished as Thomas caressed her all over. With each piece of clothing that dropped from her body, so did her fears. She dove in, allowing the passion that Thomas stirred up in her to emerge. The initial entrance of his very erect penis into the moist opening between her legs was barely painful. He knew exactly how to work his way in gently. He masterfully distracted her by kissing her hard and passionately on the lips, then more softly on her neck all the way down to her shoulders. Thomas was very gentle and careful with her.

Because of him, the monumental experience of her life, which she had always thought would be scary and painful, was the most pleasurable and unforgettable she would ever know. So much so, that she easily welcomed rounds two and three that followed.

Almost a week had gone by after the party, there was still no word from Thomas—a preemptive sign that Lydia ignored. It goes without saying that Lydia was a total basket case, as any woman would have been in her position. Sandra tried to help Lydia accept the night she spent with Thomas as the one-night stand that it obviously was. "Get over it and move on," she said.

Lydia wouldn't hear of it though. Something special, besides losing her virginity, took place on that night she spent with Thomas. She fell in love. And, he fell in love with her—at least that's what she told herself.

Then, just as everyone was telling her what a fool she was making of herself, holding out for him to reappear, he suddenly did. Strangely, he didn't offer an explanation for his whereabouts, but Lydia was too captivated by the bouquet of red roses and her newfound feelings of love to care. She was just glad he was back.

From that day forward, Lydia and Thomas were inseparable. Soon after, a new Lydia began to emerge much to the surprise of herself and her friends. She was finally coming into her own as a woman with Thomas in her life.

Before she began dating Thomas, Lydia had been all work and no play. She concentrated on her schoolwork—getting straight A's and ensured her chances for a full scholarship to college. Just as she and her mother planned, Lydia graduated from one of the most challenging high schools in the city with highest honors.

With hard work and discipline, she managed to maintain the same academic success in college, except freshman year. Lydia was so focused on her studies that she also didn't give much thought to her appearance. Unlike her friends, Lydia downplayed her femininity, preferring to wear loose-fitting jeans and oversized shirts. She did whatever she had to do to divert the attention of the prowling guys on campus, who would've only interfered with her educational and career goals.

When Thomas entered her life, the sensual and sexy woman within Lydia broke free! She started showing off her well toned body by wearing halter-tops, belly shirts, and fitted jeans. Her shoulder-length hair, usually pulled back into a neat ponytail, and cinched with a scrunchie, was eventually cut and styled into long, cascading, colored layers. In a matter of months, Lydia had transformed into a completely different woman.

Just as easily as Thomas slipped into her life and turned it upside down, he exited pretty much the same way. Only worse. He took her innocence and shattered her dreams of happily ever after. It had seemed that everything was going smoothly between them. Then one day, two and a half months later, Thomas dropped a bomb on her out of the clear blue sky. He'd changed the plans they'd discussed about him leaving the military and enrolling in college. Instead, he reenlisted for another four years.

Lydia was speechless. She demanded an explanation. She needed one. They hadn't discussed marriage or anything like that, but she definitely thought they were headed in that direction. Obviously, she was wrong. Thomas said they were moving too fast, and that maybe the distance would help them to be sure that what they had was real. Two weeks later, he was gone, leaving Lydia crushed and devastated.

That would prove to be only one of the many disappearing acts that Thomas would pull. During his years in the military, he bounced in and out of Lydia's life, each time, promising a future for them. And each time, Lydia would stop whatever she had going on, and buy into whatever he was selling, only to be left looking like a fool in the end.

Lydia felt like damaged goods by the time she started to realize there would be nothing between her and Thomas. She couldn't believe she had allowed herself to be played for a fool. After that experience, the last thing she wanted was to be bothered with men. She concluded that her judgment was all wrong in that area, or she wouldn't have been so dead wrong about Thomas. So she devised a plan to focus on her career, family and friends, and stay away from the dating scene. When she did date, she made sure it was on her terms. That way if she found out that someone wasn't worth her time, or had a girlfriend or worse: a wife, she wouldn't be stunned and heartbroken. She'd simply cut her losses early. And when guys were trying to get too close to her, she would avoid them, until they got the picture and left her alone.

Her plan was working just fine for her, until Roy came back on the scene. Before she and Roy started seeing each other again, Lydia had rarely dated, preferring to spend her free time with her girlfriends, her mom, or at networking events. That was the way she liked it. But Roy wasn't having it.

Roy pursued Lydia with full knowledge of her history with Thomas, having the inside scoop through Sandra. He had the perfect strategy concocted before Sandra reunited them on their "surprise" double date. Choosing the friend role, Roy settled for long conversations on the phone, Saturday night at the movies, or double dating with Sandra and Lester. He never tried to pressure Lydia into a relationship. Instead, he took a slow, steady approach to her heart. He knew from the beginning a relationship between them would happen eventually.

He was right. Before Lydia knew what happened, she found herself looking forward to talking to Roy every morning before work and at night before bed. She relished in the attention he gave her. Lydia did something she didn't think was possible. She fell in love again. And it felt more real than anything she had ever experienced with Thomas.

So why was she risking such a good thing with Roy, only to play the same game with Thomas. Maybe she was stupid or plain crazy. Lydia was only sure about one thing. There was no way she could move on completely with Roy, or anyone else, until she put a final finish to this thing with Thomas.

Steadying her fingers on her computer keyboard, she began typing.:

Thomas,

By now I've realized that you are full of shit. I'm done playing these games with you. You've had every

chance to be with me, but you've always left when things got too close. I deserve better than that. I deserve better than you...

Truly not yours,

Lydia

SIX

A untie Liddy!" Alicia shouted as she scurried, excitedly toward Lydia, who'd just entered the family room of the Alexander home with Sandra. Alicia slammed smack into Lydia's stomach, wrapping her little arms around Lydia's waist. Alicia was squeezing Lydia with all of her might, as though she hadn't just seen her last weekend. Alicia was extra excited to be spending the entire weekend with Lydia. It had been over a month since the two of them had their usual quality time together. While Lydia had been preparing for her presentation at work, she hadn't had as much time to give Alicia.

So Lydia hugged her back, warmly, showing equal excitement. "Hi, sweetheart," she smiled, planting a kiss on top of Alicia's head. I've missed you soooo much," she said emphatically.

"Me too, Auntie. Can we go now?" Alicia asked excitedly.

"My goodness, Alicia," Sandra interjected. "You don't have to be *that* happy to be leaving your mommy all by herself for the night." Sandra pretended to pout.

Quickly, Alicia dashed to her mother's side, hugging her around the legs. "Ohh, Mommy, you have me all the time. Plus, Daddy will be here with you. I have to spend time with Auntie Liddy, because she's always by herself." How mature the six-year-old sounded! Neither Sandra nor Lydia could resist smiling.

Pretending to ponder over Alicia's explanation, Sandra finally said, "Alright. But only because it's just for one night. Okay?"

Alicia was gleaming, nodding in agreement. "So, we can go?" Alicia asked again, a little less enthusiastically, for her mother's sake.

"Sure, honey. Go get your things from your bedroom." As Alicia ran towards the stairs, Sandra called out in her parental tone, "Make sure those toys are off the floor before you come down."
Sandra and Lydia sat on the couch. "Sometimes I swear that girl wishes you were her mother. She doesn't get that happy when she's with me."

"I'm not the one who spanks her." They both laughed.

"You know, right now that little girl is my only source of happiness," Sandra said, seriously. "It's kind of hard for me to let her go, but I know the tension in the house is not good for her, either. It'll do her good to get out."

Lydia smiled consolingly at her friend. "I'm sure it'll do you good, too, having some time to yourself to really sort things out."

Sandra's menstrual cycle was two weeks late. She didn't need a doctor's visit to confirm that she was pregnant. Her cycle had always been like clockwork, every twenty-eight days. The problem was that, for the first time in her marriage, she was strongly considering filing for divorce from Lester.

They'd been married for eight years. He'd cheated during most of them. But Sandra had coped, convincing herself that dealing with Lester's "habit" was worth the life of privilege and wealth that he provided for her and Alicia, and the other children she planned on having. Until his most recent affair turned into a fatal attraction, Lester had done an almost excellent job of shielding Sandra from the other women. With the exception of one or two late nights coming home and the impromptu weekend business trips, Lester was the picturesque husband and father. He and Sandra enjoyed many private romantic dinners for two. There were family weekend trips to Mackinaw Island, Michigan Adventure, and Great Lakes Lodge, the yearly trip to Disney World, Six Flags in Atlanta, and the like. And Lester was always showering his girls, Sandra and Alicia, with small and big gifts to their hearts' delights. Sandra had always rationalized that with all that he did for her and Alicia, the time Lester spent with his mistresses couldn't have been anything of significance.

Clearly this last woman, who Sandra later came to know as Felicia Goins, considered her relationship with Lester *very* significant. She went ballistic when Lester tried to break things off with her. Unlike the other women Lester fooled around with, this woman refused to go away quietly. The crazed woman began prank calling the house and shouting obscenities at Sandra. Felicia even managed to get Sandra's cell phone number. She made so many calls to the Alexander home and Sandra's cell phone that Sandra had to have both numbers changed.

The insanity continued for almost two weeks until about a week and a half ago when Felicia caught Sandra by surprise. She was waiting beside Sandra's car as she was dropping Alicia off at her dance class. The encounter was nothing like Sandra had imagined. Felicia apologized for her psychotic behavior, explaining that Lester had deceived her by telling her that he and Sandra were separated and preparing to file for divorce, because he knew she wouldn't have anything to do with a married man. He'd been pursuing her for months, and she had finally given in about six months ago. Then, abruptly, he had dumped her—saying that Sandra wanted him back and was holding their daughter as ammunition to keep him from going through with the divorce!

Felicia realized that Lester was just another married man full of shit, but she had some news of her own. She was pregnant. Candidly, she told Sandra, as she had Lester, that she was keeping the baby, and had every intention of filing for financial support.

It was an understatement to say there were heavy issues in the Alexander household. Although Sandra tried to keep everything from Alicia, it was unrealistic to think that Alicia wouldn't be affected at all. As a matter of fact, late one night, awakened by her parent's arguing, Alicia called Lydia, asking to be picked up. Instead, Lydia read her a few pages from one of her favorite books until she heard Alicia's sleepy breathing.

Alicia assured Sandra that her room was in perfect condition when she came back downstairs. After hugging and kissing her mom, she hurriedly skipped outside to Lydia's truck to put her things inside. Before departing, Lydia gave Sandra a strong, gentle hug of encouragement and support.

A typical six-year-old, Alicia was a chatter box if Lydia ever knew one, bless her little heart. But Lydia never tired of the energy and enthusiasm expelled from Alicia. By the end of the twenty-minute ride from Sandra's upscale suburban home in Farmington Hills, Lydia had been brought completely up to speed on every important issue that mattered to Alicia—summer camp, Girl Scouts, her five best friends at school, and so on. A game of Eye-Spy entertained them for the rest of the ride to Lydia's house.

In record time, they arrived at Lydia's home: a modest three-bedroom Colonial style home in a quiet neighborhood on Detroit's west side. Lydia couldn't get the front door closed fast enough before Alicia darted off to the guest room, which pretty much belonged to her, since she was the only company Lydia had who stayed overnight.

For the first few hours they enjoyed their usual—which Alicia never seemed to tire of—eating pizza and popcorn, and snacking on Lydia's freshly baked chocolate walnut brownies while watching Alicia's favorite Disney Channel programs. Since there weren't many positive programs for children on television, Lydia was thankful for the Disney Channel, which showcased positive programs for children. Her and Alicia's favorites were *That's So Raven, The Proud Family, and Sister, Sister*, which featured African American families. It wasn't until well after midnight that Lydia carried a sleeping Alicia to her bed.

No sooner than she had tucked Alicia into the futon-style bed, her telephone began ringing. Since Alicia was a light sleeper, same as her, Lydia made a quick dash to the phone to keep it from making it to a third ring. *Psst!* Dead air. Again. It was the third or fourth prank call she'd had in the last couple of days. Boy had she picked the wrong time to downsize her phone service, removing the Caller ID. She'd love to curse out whoever was playing on her phone. Lydia made a mental note to get the tracking service back ASAP, if the calls persisted

In the morning, over sweet blueberry pancakes, Alicia asked, "Auntie, why are my mommy and daddy fighting? Is my daddy bad?"

"Ouch!" Lydia winced. She knew that Alicia was well aware that her parents were having problems, but she had hoped she and Alicia could get through the weekend without any such inquiries. Clearly, she wasn't that lucky. On the other hand, Lydia couldn't help feeling grateful that Alicia felt close enough to her to trust her with her questions.

Lydia wasn't sure how to address the question. It wasn't like she was anywhere near an expert on marital issues, let alone helping a child cope with them. Giving it her best shot, she began carefully. "Well, honey, sometimes people who love each other go through times when they don't get along. After a little time, they remember how much they love each other, then things usually go back to normal."

"What happens if they don't?" Alicia asked as the pride Lydia felt from her response quickly disappeared.

Damn. Lydia cursed under her breath. Kids certainly aren't afraid to ask questions that were on their, most-times, too inquisitive minds. But maybe that isn't so bad, considering there is so much going on in the world that kids need to be aware of for their own safety.

Nevertheless, Lydia wasn't the one who Alicia should be having this serious conversation with. That was for her mom and dad. "I've got an idea," Lydia smiled, beginning to clear the dishes off the table. "Let's go visit your favorite grandma!" No amount of concerns about her parents would make Alicia turn down that suggestion.

They spent the rest of the day with Lydia's mother. They shopped and ate lunch at the Rainforest Café, a popular restaurant located in Great Lakes Crossing Mall, one of the largest and newest malls in Auburn Hills. It was one of Lydia and her mother's favorite hang outs. The mall was so huge, it had taken Lydia and her mother about four visits before they'd finally covered its entirety.

If Lydia was guilty of spoiling Alicia, her mother was even more so. Alicia was the closest thing to a grandchild that she had, and she never got tired of reminding Lydia of it. Needless to say, Alicia cleaned up royally on her weekends with Lydia.

After they finished shopping, Lydia and Alicia dropped her mother back off, and then they stopped at the drive-in for a double feature, during which both of them fell asleep. Alicia remained asleep on the drive home.

"Alicia," Lydia called, trying to wake the heavily sleeping child, who didn't stir at all, until she called her the third time. It was close to useless, though, as sluggishly as the child was moving. The outside of her house was completely dark, except for a tiny speck of light from her neighbor's backyard that spilled over into her driveway. It was a quick reminder of the "dusk to dawn" light her mother had been advising her to have installed so she wouldn't have to worry about forgetting to leave the porch light on. Which was exactly the case tonight. She hadn't planned to be gone so long when she and Alicia had left the house earlier that afternoon. Now here it was almost two o'clock in the morning, and she was loaded down with several shopping bags and Alicia.

Moving swiftly, Lydia grabbed the bags from the back seat of her truck, while waking Alicia. "Come on, sweetie, let's get in the house." Grudgingly, Alicia opened her eyes, and complied with Lydia's words.

They rounded the recently trimmed bushes surrounding her front porch.

"*What's that?*" Lydia thought, slowing her steps. Behind them, she thought she heard a noise in the otherwise silent night. Footsteps, maybe. Of course, she wasn't waiting to confirm her suspicion. Using her better judgment, she quickened her steps, pulling Alicia alongside of her. Hurriedly, she forced her key into the front door lock. When it unlatched, she and Alicia moved quickly inside. Lydia turned to close and double lock the door. But, just as she was closing the door, she was shaken by a leather gloved hand reaching inside.

Lydia reached for the large pipe wrench she kept in the corner behind her entrance door for protection, when an all-too familiar voice called out to her, "It's me, Lydia. Thomas."

His sudden appearance startled Lydia. Not enough, though, for her to not take notice of how exceptionally gorgeous and sexy Thomas was, coolly dressed in a dark blue pair of baggy Sean Jean jeans, and an oversized button-down shirt. Shamefully, a flash of her undressing him passed through her mind and she felt her body respond with a twinge of desire, as though they'd just been together yesterday. Quickly, though, she forced those thoughts out of her mind.

"Thomas, what the hell are you doing here?" She spat, angrily.

"Who's that, Auntie Liddy?" Alicia asked, quietly, peeking her head from behind Lydia's leg. Lydia quickly turned her attention to an inquisitive looking Alicia.

"Nobody, honey. Take these bags upstairs. Right now," she added sternly when Alicia didn't get moving along fast enough.

When she was sure Alicia was out of earshot, Lydia stepped outside the door. Planting her hands on her hips, she said again, but more sternly, "What are you doing here?"

Thomas was calm, completely unmoved by her obvious anger. He moved in closer to her, making her eyes nervously avoid his. "If I'm not mistaken, you did say you needed to see how serious I was—so here I am."

She couldn't believe what she'd just heard—like she was supposed to be impressed or something. Rolling her eyes, she replied, "Yeah, well, I also remember telling you that I didn't want to see you for a while. And now, here you are, completely disregarding what I asked. Besides, you can see, I'm busy—so I need you to leave."

"Come on," Thomas pressed, sounding all Rico Suave cool. "I'm trying to show you how serious I am about this. You and me."

"While I can appreciate your efforts, this is not the time. So consider yourself dismissed. Next time call to see if you're welcomed, so you don't waste your time or mine," Lydia walked away coldly, turning her back to him. After one final glare for added emphasis, Lydia resolutely closed the door in his face.

Ruthless satisfaction was mounting within her as she peeked through the picture window of her home to watch a bewildered Thomas tread slowly to his car, a sharp winter white Lincoln Navigator, her favorite luxury SUV. Though she felt a twinge of guilt coming over her, she relinquished it quickly, having no room for the old, softy, sucka' for love Lydia to resurface.

The coldness with which Thomas had treated her in the past forced Lydia to travel a less foolish road with him. When she and Thomas were together, she'd always put herself at his beck and call. It was all about him. Making him happy was all that mattered to her.

It was a new day, she declared to herself, as she finally turned away from the window. Thomas had just encountered his first dose of the new Lydia.

SEVEN

W hat the hell just happened?" Thomas asked himself as he merged onto Eastbound I-94 back towards his rented house the military had set him up in as temporary housing. His head was still spinning from that totally unexpected reception, or lack thereof, he had received from Lydia. He'd been caught completely off guard.

Getting back into Lydia's good graces was going to be more of a challenge than he had initially thought. If he didn't know that from her unresponsiveness to his e-mails, there was certainly no doubt now.

He couldn't really blame her, considering the way he had treated her. In fact, he was more surprised that it had taken her this long to toughen up a bit towards him, after all the coldhearted, bullshit he'd dished out over the years. No one knew more than he did how sorry he was to have hurt her. She really was the woman he had always wanted to be with. He knew it from the moment he took her virginity.

Sometimes things happen that are out of your control, to reroute the course of your life. And it takes a man to take back that control. Last year, Thomas made the decision to do just that. The first part of his plan was not reenlisting in the military. Next was to get back to the place in Lydia's heart that he knew was just for him.

He had had enough of being tugged at like a puppet on somebody else's stage. Yes, he stood to lose a lot by choosing to follow his own direction. But it was long overdue. Without a doubt, Lydia was worth the risk.

Thomas was ready to get things back on track in his life, and to right his past wrongs against Lydia. He was determined to be the man she deserved. He'd been living in what seemed like a prison for the last eight years, and he knew Lydia had been, too. They were meant to be together.

A grin crossed his lips as he remembered how many times she had called them soulmates. He was sure she still felt that way. They were great together. From the looks of it, Thomas was going to have to put in some work to help Lydia remember that, and to remember the love she had for him. That love would be his ticket inside.

Thomas sat in his truck hatching his next plan of action to penetrate Lydia's newfound shield of armor. Little did he know that behind the doors of his own home, another plan of action was being hatched.

Lydia was so unnerved by Thomas's unexpected arrival at her house that she could hardly sleep. After tossing and turning until nearly three in the morning, she knew that she and Alicia would not be making it to eight o'clock church service the next morning with her mother. So, when she dragged herself out of the bed, she left her mother a message of apologies and promised that she and Alicia would be over for dinner later that evening.

The enticing aroma of Caroline juicy, tender pot roast made Lydia's stomach growl in greedy anticipation. She and Alicia hurried up the walkway, fighting against the brisk coolness of the air on this bright Sunday afternoon. Even though her mother, who'd always been a great cook, was coming around slowly to eating healthier, Lydia still enjoyed the great traditional Sunday dinners she prepared most Sundays, usually consisting of a savory meat dish, with mashed potatoes and gravy, green beans or collard greens, or macaroni and cheese. All topped off with a decadent dessert like cream cheese pound cake.

Lydia still had a key to her mother's house. But out of respect for her mother's recent marriage to her longtime friend and Deacon at her church, George Duncan, Lydia reserved her key for emergencies only. And no matter how many times her mother and George welcomed her to use it as she pleased, she would continue to do so. The last thing Lydia wanted was to be an intruding adult child causing problems in a new marriage.

George greeted her and Alicia first, with outstretched arms as usual. "God bless you, Lydia. It's good to see you again," he chimed joyfully, embracing her. "You too, Alicia," he added, lifting her high off the ground in a circular motion, sending her into a round of giggles. A tall, robust man, George was still attractive for a man in his mid-sixties. And he could always be found with a welcoming smile on his face.

Her mother got a pretty good catch.

"How's everything been, Deacon?" Lydia asked as they walked through the living room towards the kitchen. Since her mother and George's union had been so sudden and not that long ago, Lydia wasn't sure what she was supposed to call him. She settled with "Deacon" since that's what she'd been calling him since she was a little girl attending the church with her mother.

George smiled genuinely as he replied. "The Lord is truly blessing the house of Greater Kingdom. We received a donation from Wal-Mart Corporation in the amount of ten thousand dollars for our building fund. Hallelujah!" he shouted. "And the Deacons' Ministry was able to raise two thousand dollars from our fundraiser last week to donate to the National Heart Disease Foundation. I tell you, Lydia, you should have been there. The spirit was sho-nuff moving in the house when the pastor made those announcements."

"Yes indeed, it was a beautiful sight," Caroline joined in, once they entered the kitchen. Lydia was just about to hug her mother when Alicia sprinted ahead of her, cutting her off.

"Grandma Carol," Alicia yelped, running to Caroline with open arms. "I missed you since yesterday."

Planting a big fat, grandma-like kiss on her forehead, Caroline hugged her back. "I. Missed. You. Too," Caroline said, emphasizing each word.

Lydia apologized again for not making it to church that morning. Since moving back home after college, she always attended church services with her mother. At first, it was at her mother's urging.

"It's important to have a place of worship that you belong to and attend if you're going to stay grounded in God's word," her mother had told her often while she was away at college. Caroline had even mailed Lydia a list of churches near campus, so she'd have no excuse. But, like many college students, Lydia did stray, until the first time Thomas broke her heart.

When she ran to her mother crying like a baby, her mother explained to her, tenderly, "God uses the tribulation in your life to make you stronger, to bring you closer to Him. A lot of times that's the only time His children call on Him." Lydia always remembered those words.

How right her mother had been! Lydia couldn't get through the doors of the church fast enough! And she stayed until her broken heart managed to mend to some point of normality. Then she slacked off in her attendance again.

It was her mother's diagnosis with breast cancer five years ago that forced Lydia's hand with her spiritual commitment. Though the doctors were hopeful about her mother's survival chances, Lydia knew that only the Lord could heal her mother. So when God answered her prayers by making her mother a breast cancer survivor, Lydia made a promise to rejoin her mother's church and attend faithfully. Besides the occasional slip ups, Lydia held true to her promise.

Dinner was getting under way when Lydia noticed an extra setting at the table. Before she could question who it was for, the doorbell rang. George had already made a dash for the door.

"You guys expecting more company, Ma?" Lydia asked. Caroline didn't have a chance to respond before George reentered the dining room, followed by Roy. Lydia was surprised, and nearly choked on the forkful of green beans she had just put in her mouth.

"Uhm, Roy, what are you doing here?" Lydia asked incredulously, trying desperately to hide the quiver in her voice.

"I was invited," Roy replied, deliberately avoiding her eyes. He greeted Caroline with a loving hug before taking the seat directly across from her. "It's good to see you, too," his voice reeked of sarcasm. "Hey cutie," he said sweetly to his little cousin, squeezing her cheeks softly. Alicia smiled in return, but couldn't speak, as she was concentrating on eating the scrumptious food before her.

It was beyond impossible for Lydia to pretend she wasn't affected by Roy's presence. In fact, she was quite pissed off. The nerve of George and her mother to sit with her all this time and not say anything about this obviously planned dinner guest!

They weren't fooling anybody. She knew what this was all about. It was her mother's indiscreet way of showing Lydia that she was against her breakup with Roy. But, *dammit*, it was nobody's business but hers and Roy's. Obviously, no one respected that. How dare they!

If this wasn't an obvious display of her mother's disapproval of her decision to break up with Roy, Lydia didn't know what it was.

The discomfort must have clearly shown on her face because Alicia asked, "What's wrong, Auntie?"

Lydia looked at Alicia lovingly. "Nothing sweetie. I'm just tired from last night. That's all."

"Because of that man who scared us last night?" Alicia said horridly. *Could she have said anything worse?* If there was ever a time Lydia could've put some tape over the Alicia's mouth, this would've been it. Before Lydia could counter Alicia's overzealous comment, Caroline was already on her feet.

"My God! What man?" Caroline asked, frightened. Roy was silent, but concern poured through his eyes.

"Oh, Ma, it was nothing. Somebody mistook my house for one of my neighbors. We were just a little…"

"I thought you called him Thomas, Auntie," reminded Alicia. Lydia's stomach began to sink deeper and deeper. Apparently, there was no end to Alicia's untimely comments.

"No, I didn't," Lydia said sharply and more sternly than intended. "You must have misunderstood. Finish eating so I can get you home." Turning her attention to the concerned expressions of everyone, she added.

"Like I said, it was nothing to be concerned about."

Alicia silently continued eating her dinner. Flushed with guilt, Lydia knew she was wrong for doing that to Alicia. What choice did she really have? No way in the world could she admit to Thomas being at her house last night. She cringed at the sheer thought of it. Her appetite lost, Lydia excused herself from the table. She needed to regroup. The bathroom was the perfect place.

The reflection facing her in the mirror was horrifying—mirroring how she felt on the inside. Perspiration formed on her brow, and her skin flushed. The guilt she saw in her own eyes was too much to handle. Thomas had only been around for less than a month, and she was already lying to the people closest to her. But telling them the truth was not an option. At least not right now. She needed to handle this situation with Thomas on her own before her family and friends involved their two cents.

Exiting the bathroom, Lydia was startled to find Roy blocking her path. Their eyes met, but the silence between them was short.

"So the truth comes out, huh, Lydia," Roy stated flatly. His lean six-four frame towered over her. He was standing close enough for the sexy scent of his Sean Jean cologne to send an embarrassing chill through her body. He'd just left the barbershop—his goatee was perfect, as was his faded hair cut. Though his eyes were angry, he couldn't have been more attractive.

Lydia nervously averted her eyes from his confident gaze. "You shouldn't even be here, Roy," she said. She tried to push past him, but he wouldn't have it.

"I guess it's a good thing that wasn't your choice. Now don't ignore my question." His tone was more demanding, dripping with controlled anger.

"Look, Tho… uhm, Roy." *That little slip-up didn't help matters.* This was way more than she bargained for. She had to get out of here. "Roy, all I can say is that it's not what you think…"

"Oh, it's not, huh? Roy interrupted her. "You want me to believe it's just coincidental that after you break up with me, Thomas is back on the scene?" He shook his head, disgusted. "Then you try to confuse a little kid about what she heard, just to cover for yourself." Abruptly, Roy stopped talking, giving thought to his next words. "I guess it was for the best that you dumped me. I need someone who knows what the hell they want. And you obviously don't." Before turning to walk away he added coldly, "Just don't call me when you discover that he's never going to be anything more than what he's always been."

Tears formed immediately in her eyes, but she fought to keep them from falling. Gathering herself as best she could, Lydia stormed into the living room, where Roy had joined her mother and George.

"Come on Alicia, honey. It's time to go. Give grandma a kiss." Alicia appeared sad, but she complied. Lydia could see the concern and questions across her mother's face. Lydia gave her a quick hug, whispering while carefully avoiding Roy's eyes, "Everything's fine, Ma. I'll call you later."

EIGHT

L ydia's weekend had gotten off to such a great start, beginning with the presentation going over so well, fun time with Alicia, and then triumphantly putting Thomas in his place. But it couldn't have ended more horribly. She was unable to sleep most of the night for seeing the look of pain and disgust in Roy's eyes. She couldn't have been happier when her alarm clock sounded the next morning. She was ready for work in no time at all. Work was just the distraction she needed.

The last thing that Lydia wanted was for Roy to have the impression that she had dumped him for Thomas. It may have appeared that way, but that really wasn't the case. But would she ever be able to make him see that?

The chocolate Belgian nut flavored coffee she had been sipping on since she'd been in the office had grown cold in her "I Love NY" coffee cup she'd bought when she, Sandra, and Kania took a weekend trip to New York a couple of years ago. As much as she wanted to hide in her office for the rest of the day, her caffeine addiction drove her to the break room.

She put the employee evaluations she'd been thumbing through for the past two hours to the side of her desk. She smiled cordially at a couple of her peers and employees in route to the break room, which was filled with other coffee addicts on their second, third, and fourth cups of the morning.

Not desiring any unwanted inquiries about anything that was bothering her, Lydia put on the phoniest smile she could muster, speaking cheerfully to everyone she encountered. After refilling her cup, she quickly escaped back to her office, this time, hopefully to get some work done.

Well, it was a thought anyway. Work was the farthest thing from Lydia's mind. Her mind was thick with thoughts of Roy and Thomas. She still felt *something* when thoughts of Thomas emerged into her mind, even after he had left her, again. What those feelings were, she wasn't sure. That's what she needed to find out. And she needed to find out before she could ever promise marriage to Roy. But, considering what was no doubt going through Roy's mind after dinner at her mother's on Sunday, what Lydia wanted between herself and Roy probably didn't matter. But it still worried her.

The workday dragged as slow as a snail crossing the street. And Lydia's head was no clearer than when she awoke that morning. Even though it wasn't her usual gym day, a strenuous workout was sure to do the trick to either clear her mind or drain her so much that she couldn't do anything but crash when she got back home. So before leaving the building, Lydia made a stop to the locker she maintained at work, to retrieve her spare workout gear, then headed over to Fit Forever.

On the drive, even some of her favorite Will Downy tunes on the radio couldn't keep her mind from churning over this mess she'd let get started with Thomas. How she had ever considered that man her soul mate was beyond her. She couldn't have been more wrong. Unfortunately, no matter how wrong she was, it hadn't stopped her from letting him back into her life whenever he was ready.

Was that how the cookie crumbled when dealing with your first love? Your first sex—awesome sex! Lydia felt, like most girls, that the man you gave your virginity to had to be special. And, too, like most girls, her first love, could make her weak in the knees with just the right look.

From the look of things the other night, Thomas still had that look. A look that said, "I can have you when I want you." The fact that her stomach still did that familiar quiver at the very sight of him was scary as hell, considering that the whole idea behind her even giving him the time of day was to bring a final close to the revolving door of their relationship.

Her plan was to create a little distance between herself and Roy so she could settle things with Thomas. She had to get to the bottom of why she kept letting Thomas back into her life, when he'd proven to her time and time again that he was no good for her. Was it really something between them that no amount of heartbreak could end? Or was she just afraid to let go of a predictable past and move on with an unpredictable future with Roy, regardless of how promising it looked? Maybe being hurt by someone who's hurt you before isn't as bad as being hurt by someone new. Who was she really afraid of? Thomas? Or Roy? Either way, it was time for her to face her fear.

The sun had already begun to set when Lydia arrived at the gym that evening. It was Monday, and Fit Forever was filled with its usual crowd of exercise addicts, or at least those who loved coming to be seen at the gym. For the first time that day, a smile crossed Lydia's lips as she walked toward the women's locker room passing by mostly slender bodies and rippled muscles. She thought of what Marianne had said about the majority of the people in the gym already being in shape.

There were a couple of step aerobics classes already in progress, but Lydia wasn't in much of a mood to be in that close proximity to others. She pretty much just wanted to run as fast as she could on the treadmill and make herself so tired that all she could think of was how tired her body was, instead of all the other crap that was going on in her life.

After quickly changing into her navy Reebok sports bra, tank and shorts, Lydia scanned the room for the treadmill she would use. As Fit Forever was not lacking in the equipment department, it didn't take Lydia any time at all to find a treadmill in an ideal location, one that was in full view of the ceiling-mounted nineteen-inch television. Expertly, she input her settings on the familiar equipment to an incline level of eight, at a pace of five MPH, for a time period of fifty minutes, inclusive of her warm-up and cool down.

Lydia tuned her MP3 player to the CNN station that was playing on the television. There were plenty of interesting news topics being discussed to distract Lydia's attention from Thomas and Roy.

By the time she tired of listening to the news, Lydia could have kicked herself for being so caught up in her love life. Kids were getting shot outside of schools. Young American boys were still dying over in Iraq. It really ticked her off whenever she thought about all of the young men and women, mostly between the ages of nineteen and twenty-five, who probably joined the military to receive the college tuition benefits, but got caught up in this farce of a war that Bush started, which, coincidentally, none of his children or relatives were fighting in. That thought made her run even harder as she finished the last ten minutes of her cardio exercise.

Before she knew it, Lydia had run an additional twenty minutes, and it didn't even feel like it. Where had the time gone? Her mind was so far into the television, she had lost track of time.

It was nearing the eight o'clock hour. The usual pack of weightlifters had begun to die down. Lydia didn't fool around too much with the weights. Getting bulging muscles was never a part of her fitness goals, only maintaining her already slender frame. But just for the hell of it, she felt like pumping a little iron to see what she was made of, so to speak.

Twenty minutes later, she was finished. Feeling satisfied and content with her workout, she was ready for a little relaxation in the sauna, which signaled the official end of her workout. As she strolled at an even pace in the direction of the sauna in the pool area, through the women's locker room, she had an awkward sensation of being watched. It wasn't the normal feeling of knowing that some guy was checking her out; this felt weird. But when she turned to see who it was, she didn't notice anyone. That same creepy feeling remained when she pushed open the wooden door to the sauna. Just as the door was closing, the intrusive, nosy woman who had interrupted her and Sandra's conversation the last time came in behind her.

She was taller than Lydia, about five six, but just as slim, probably an even size six. A little too much foundation for Lydia's taste covered the woman's seemingly flawless sandy brown skin. Unlike the last time she saw her, the woman was less disheveled looking, with her long black and gold streaked hair pulled to the top of her head in a neat ponytail.

"Hey girl," the woman chimed as though they were old friends, tightening the towel around her. "I thought I saw you pounding away on that treadmill. When I saw you come in, I thought you were going to come into the aerobics class."

Lydia was completely astounded at how this woman, whom she didn't even know, was talking so comfortably to her, like they *weren't* virtual strangers. Yes, she knew there were extremely sociable people who took to other people very quickly, but for some reason, this woman gave her the creeps. In fact, stalking came to mind. Lydia wasn't going to be rude and standoffish, but she was definitely going to keep this woman at arm's length, starting with keeping her responses as short as possible.

"Just felt like doing my own thing today."

The woman missed the point, BIG TIME! She pushed forward. "Hmmm, sounds like man trouble," she cooed as a slight grin crossed her lips. Her green eyes that probably drove men crazy sparkled as she directed them at Lydia. She must have sensed Lydia's bewilderment because she suddenly became apologetic. "I'm sorry. I guess I'm being nosy again. See," she began explaining, "my husband and I, and our son just moved here from Texas and I don't know a soul. I thought I'd join a local gym to meet some people who shared a similar interest. I guess my husband is right about me coming across as pushy sometimes instead of friendly, which is really what I am."

Immediately, Lydia felt regretful about prejudging this woman as some kind of lunatic when all she was guilty of was trying to make a friend.

"No, I'm the one who should be apologizing. It's got to be hard moving from your hometown to a big city like Detroit and not knowing anyone. My husband would have to tie me down along with the luggage to get me to move from all of my familiarity."

The woman's face went flat. "Oh, so you're married?"

"No. Just speaking hypothetically," Lydia answered, wrapping an extra towel around her head to keep her hair from sweating out.

"Oh, so it was your boyfriend who put you in a funky mood today, huh?" the woman pressed on.

There's that nosiness again, Lydia thought, but didn't say. Instead, she responded kindly. "Not quite, but it's nothing I'd like to discuss. I actually came in this evening to get my mind off of some things. For awhile, at least."

"Oops. There I go again. All in your business and we don't even know each other's names. I'm Angelina," she finally introduced herself. Angelina had a pretty enough face, but those beautiful green eyes set the stage. With such a tantalizing look, Lydia figured Angelina for one of those women whose looks had gotten them just about everything they'd wanted. Lydia could also see that the looks were beginning to fade, but that Angelina would be the last to realize it.

Another important detail, too, was that Angelina did not have the look of a happy woman. Maybe it was the recent move. Or perhaps the marriage. Whatever it was, Lydia decided to be a little softer and friendlier to Angelina.

Extending her hand to welcome Angelina's, Lydia smiled. "I'm Lydia. Now we'll be able to put names with faces the next time we see each other," she said getting up to leave.

"Will you be here the next time with your friend who was with you last week?" Angelina asked.

More inquiries, Lydia thought, pushing her annoyance far behind her. Obviously, Angelina was trying to connect, a little too hard. "That's somewhat unpredictable, but I'm here pretty regularly," Lydia returned through a semi- forced smile. At the door, before exiting, Lydia said, "It was nice meeting you, Angelina. I'll see you around."

The door closed as Angelina was saying goodbye. Fearing the meddlesome woman was going to try to leave with her, too, Lydia made a swift run to the locker room, showered, and then quickly threw on her clothes. Once at her truck, that eerie feeling of being watched returned. And sure enough, when she pulled out of the parking lot, she could see Angelina standing at the doorway, overzealously waving in her direction.

NINE

L ying awake in bed, Thomas stared blankly at the stucco ceiling above him. He wasn't sure how long he'd been awake, but the painful heaviness of his eyes clearly indicated that he hadn't slept more than a few hours, if even that. How could he have expected better after Lydia's reception toward him almost two weeks ago? Since then, it had been the only thing he could think about.

The silence in the house was not welcomed. Thomas had never been able to think in complete silence. Background noise had a way of helping his thoughts filter through his mind more clearly. So he got out of bed, quietly crept to the basement where he put on his Nike running shoes, to run a few miles on his treadmill. A good run would help him clear his head, and hopefully revealing new direction with which to break Lydia down.

An hour later, his smooth, chocolate face dripping with sweat, an idea sparked in Thomas' head. Maybe it'll work, maybe it won't, he thought. At this point, he was willing to put himself out on a limb to get what was his—Lydia.

When he was a young cat, Thomas used to think that if you could get one woman, you could get them all. Women were nothing more than toys to him, and no more than pieces of ass to get his jollies off. What else were they really good for? His own unapologetic whore of a mother and the absenteeism of any real man to tell him anything different were the reasons behind his thinking. But even with the worst he thought of women, he'd never known a woman could be as deceitful, malicious, and vindictive as the woman with whom he shared his bed. He was still trying to figure out how he let himself get suckered like this.

Thomas knew he had been selfish all the times he had reentered Lydia's life, knowing full well that he wouldn't be staying. But during those times, she was just the breath of fresh air that he needed, with all that he was going through in his life. Now he was ready for Lydia's fresh air again. And this time, he had no plans of leaving. This time, he was determined that nothing would get in his way, not even his wife.

Judging from outside appearances, Tony's Pit had the look of a rundown little dump, but it was nothing of the sort once inside the finely run establishment. The owner, Antonio, a feisty, sixty-something man took pride, as he should, in the eatery he started on his own in his early days of working for General Motors. He had been running the restaurant fulltime, with the help of his son. Tony's Pit was the cleanest, most sanitary eatery serving the best Buffalo style chicken wings in the heart of the city.

"The Pit", as it was most often referred, was packed with its usual midday lunch crowd. If Lydia and Sandra didn't plan in advance for their lunch dates, they'd be wasting all of Lydia's lunch time waiting for a table like all the other patrons who Lydia passed by. She ignored envious stares as she approached her and Sandra's favorite table by the front window only minutes after arriving. The truth was that she and Sandra did so much flirting with Antonio *and* his son that when they started coming to the Pit a few years ago, they were given a little preferential treatment, as long as they called ahead. They swore never to reveal their little secret to anyone else.

"Hey girl!" Lydia greeted Sandra smiling as she bent down to hug her before taking the seat across from her. Sandra was looking fantastic as usual, dressed in a loose-fitting red DKNY top, slim fitting black slacks, and finished off with black sling back pumps. Only three and a half months pregnant, Sandra was already complaining about her clothes fitting too snug, but she refused to buy maternity clothes until she was further into the second trimester.

"One day I'll be the skinny one while you're bursting out of your clothes whenever you get yourself knocked up," Sandra promised, when Lydia lovingly teased her about how tight a pair of jeans were that she had on. Only Sandra didn't know that Lydia couldn't wait for the day to be settled enough in her life to be in her motherhood shoes.

"I'm glad you finally got here. A few people already offered to join me, thinking I was dining alone," Sandra said after Lydia was seated.

"Chile, please. I was only running a few minutes behind schedule. You know how it goes. Some important call that can't wait, of course, comes in just as it's time to go out to lunch."

"No, actually I don't." Sandra was one of the few women Lydia knew who had the luxury, as she called it, of not working outside of the home. Lester, her politically driven, lawyer husband insisted that he needed her to be a fulltime wife and mother, and volunteer for various social events like all the other politicians' wives he was rubbing elbows with. What it was, Lydia concluded, was that he wanted him and Sandra to look the proper part of the happy, perfect family, which they couldn't have been farther away from. Not to mention, keeping Sandra at home with no independent income of her own was the best way to keep her dependent upon him. Lydia only hoped for the day when Sandra would realize that she could still be a good, supportive wife while pursuing the dream she once had of being a pediatrician. Right now, the closest thing she had to her own desires was the volunteer work she did at the Children's Hospital.

"Ahhh, my two favorite girls," Antonio chimed, delivering their food to the table as he always did whenever he could get away from managing the crew during the busy lunch time. Simultaneously, Lydia and Sandra greeted Antonio with wide grins and thanked him kindly for his special treatment.

"That man is so sweet," Lydia commented in between bites of her grilled chicken sandwich. Sandra had ordered her food for her to cut down on time. It wouldn't have mattered what she ordered for her. Between her lunches with Sandra and many dates with Roy at the Pit, she'd had everything on the menu, and everything was great. "If Antonio was just twenty years younger, I swear, he'd be my man."

Sandra burst out laughing, then returned, "Or you could just get back with Roy."

"Not even going to go there," Lydia thought to herself, feigning off irritation with the comment. Rather than falling into another one of Sandra's "you should be with Roy" traps, which, of course always led to an argument, Lydia opted to get to the nitty gritty of why she invited Sandra to lunch in the first place, besides getting her out of the house away from her marital problems. As they ate the rest of their lunch, Lydia told Sandra all about the latest encounter she had with Angelina at the gym the other day.

Lydia settled their lunch bill at the front counter while Sandra left a five-dollar tip on the table. Outside the eatery walking towards Sandra's car, Sandra responded with skepticism. "Umph. I don't know about that one, girl. She might be one to keep a wide-opened eye on, if you know what I mean," she added with a wink.

That was Lydia's first instinct, too. "But what about the being new to the city and everything?" Lydia wanted to know.

Sandra shook her head profusely. "I don't give a *damn* if she were new to the United States of America," she said emphatically. "A normal woman doesn't push up on another woman like that in hopes of making an acquaintance unless there's something else to it. You know like, maybe she's coming from *that* other angle," she concluded.

"Ahhh, I don't know about…," Lydia was interrupted by the ringing of her cell phone. The caller ID displayed "restricted" across the screen. Normally, Lydia didn't answer those calls, but in light of the decision for the senior management position approaching, she was making it a point to answer all calls.

"Hello, Lydia Love," she announced professionally into the phone. Dead air. She said hello again, fighting off the anger rising within her. This call was just like the hang up calls she'd been receiving at home for the past few weeks. Angrily, she mashed down the "end" button until the display read "call ended." Her frustration couldn't be masked.

"What was that all about?" Sandra asked when they reached her car parked at a meter that was one line away from expiring. Lydia explained the hang up calls at home and now this one on her cell phone. This was Sandra's first time hearing about the calls, but she wasn't too concerned. "I'm sure it's no big deal. Now if you had a husband or a man at home, you might have something to be worried about with these crazy women out here running around trying to take them," Sandra said, alluding more to her own situation. Before Sandra drove off, she reminded Lydia of the fundraising dinner and art exhibit this coming weekend that she was hosting that Lydia promised to attend with her.

Back at work, Lydia didn't have time to give any more thought to the hang up calls she'd been receiving

or anything else for that matter. A major server for the Midwest region lost power and thousands of their customers were in danger of losing their service. While the network folks were humping to resolve the problem, the call center was overflowing with calls from thousands of angry customers on cell phones, mostly demanding to speak with managers to vent their frustration at what they described as "a joke of a service." It wasn't the sort of distraction Lydia had hoped for, but it did succeed in keeping her mind well off of Thomas, Roy, and prank calls.

The clock on her dashboard read six-thirty when Lydia snapped her seatbelt into place. No sooner than she pulled out of the lot did Keith Sweat's whining voice start belting out one of her favorite, although bittersweet, old school jams, *Make It Last Forever*. Lydia was floored. Just like it had always done, the song took her back to the time when Thomas disappeared on her, the first time, without any warning. She was crying her eyes out as that song played over and over again, while Sandra insensitively advised her, "Be glad the loser is gone!"

Why couldn't she just get over him like Sandra and so many others had suggested, Lydia wondered as Keith Sweat continued crooning out the reminiscent lyrics. Maybe the time had finally come, she thought as she smiled, remembering the strength she conjured up when she turned Thomas away when he popped up at her house. Then, for a moment, she thought dreadfully, "What if I'm not ready to let go?"

She shook the thoughts away. There was no time to focus on Thomas right now, her stomach reminded her as it growled loudly. She hadn't eaten anything since lunch. And as tired as she was, cooking was out of the question. Lydia scrolled through the list of phone numbers stored in her cell phone contact list until she came across the China One near her house. Before she began dialing, her phone notified her of a voice message. Might as well check it now, she decided. If she didn't, the message could go unheard for days, even weeks. More than likely it was Sandra, Lydia figured, until she heard Thomas' voice begin pouring through.

"I get it, Lydia. After everything I've put you through, you don't plan to make it easy for me to come back. I understand that. I also understand that that's going to take some action on my part. Well, there's no time like the present for me to show you that I mean business. I'll see you at your house at seven."

Oh no he didn't! Lydia thought furiously, unconsciously pressing harder on the accelerator. Even this nerve was beyond him. Especially after the last incident of him coming to her house. The remaining ten minutes to her house was cut down to about seven as she allowed her rising anger to guide her.

Her tires screeched as she came to an abrupt stop in her driveway. She was on her way to going straight ballistic if Thomas was not bluffing and was actually at her house. But when she started up her walkway her breath was instantly taken away. Red and white rose petals were sprinkled across her front lawn, all along the path to her front porch steps. Finishing off the display was a bouquet of red and white balloons attached to her front doorknob with a card with familiar handwriting stuck to one of the balloons.

Lydia,

Please accept this small gesture of my sincere apologies for taking your love for granted for so long. It is my heart's desire to spend the rest of my life making sure you never hurt because of me again.
Love always, Thomas

An unwilling smile crossed her lips. Some of the better times she'd spent with Thomas came rushing back to her. Their first Valentine's Day, in particular. Thomas had told her he didn't celebrate those kinds of man-made holidays, so she shouldn't expect anything from him. Lydia remembered being disappointed, but like Thomas also said, "Everyday should be a Happy Valentine's Day if you're with the person you love." So she tried to buy into the rationale of thinking, for Thomas' sake. Then on Valentine's Day morning, Lydia was instantly in tears when she awoke to a bed covered with rose petals.

Thomas served her breakfast in bed, too. "You're special enough to me for me to step outside of my beliefs to satisfy the love of my life," he said to her.

A white van pulling in front of her house brought her back to the present. After eyeing it suspiciously, not recognizing it, she turned to enter her house.

"Delivery for Lydia Love," an elderly, salt and pepper haired man called out. Before she responded, she noticed three slightly younger men, two black, one white, emerging from the side door of the van. They were all dressed in black and white.

"Uhm, excuse me," Lydia began. "What is all of this?" she asked. "I think you guys have the wrong address or something." The older of the men, clearly the one in charge, pulled a piece of paper from his front shirt pocket. Seconds later, nodding confirmation, he returned, "Yes, ma'am. This is the right address. The order was called in by a Mr. Thomas Cunningham, to be delivered promptly at seven-thirty. Everything's been paid for."

Lydia argued no further, stepping out of their way. After the deliverymen departed, Lydia's house was filled with the scrumptious aroma of roasted Cornish hen, red-skinned potatoes, and steamed broccoli and carrots. Her mouth watered with anticipatory delight, at the same time fearing what the night with Thomas would bring.

By seven forty-five, there was no sign of Thomas. Just as the thought was passing through her mind that this was just the kind of stunt Thomas would pull, the doorbell chimed.

Walking toward the door, she wished he was pulling one of his stunts. If she were in her right mind, she'd just let the doorbell keep ringing and ringing and ringing. Thomas had caught her completely off guard, and that definitely wasn't how she had intended to deal with him this time around. Still, she opened the door.

"Hello beautiful," he said suavely, confidently. Thomas was dressed casually in a white pants suit. His head was clean-shaven, skin smooth to the touch and easy on the eyes.

The anger Lydia had felt earlier was nowhere to be found. She'd been swept off her feet just that easily.

Opening the door fully, she waved him in. Thomas kissed her lightly on the cheek. "Everything is lovely, Thomas," she admitted, her smile wider than intended. "You've outdone yourself. I'm impressed," she added.

Closing the door behind her, Lydia leaned her body against it. Thomas turned to face her, taking in her deliciousness with his eyes, until they finally reached hers. In the few minutes that passed, they held each others' eyes intensely, the memory of the long-lasting passion they once shared resurfaced, lingering in the open space between them. The night ahead was looking to be much more than Lydia expected.

TEN

✦

Everything about dinner was delicious, from the Cornish hen to the dinner rolls. Lydia's mouth salivated with each bite taken—but not more than when Thomas ravished her neck with tender, wet kisses, as his forefinger swirled around inside her, causing her to moan softly. From the moment they sat down at the table across from each other, it became inevitable that the night would end with some serious physical contact.

Lydia couldn't believe this was happening! It was like she was standing outside of herself watching this display of animal-like passion between them. It had been quite a few months since she'd had sex. She and Roy had spent the last six months of their relationship practicing abstinence. Though the idea was more Roy's idea as he was growing in his spirituality, Lydia conceded, not knowing how hard it would be to abstain from something you've been used to getting on the regular. Yes, their bond was growing, but there were times that she wanted to feel the warmth of his body against hers. But she never tried to tempt him.

But Thomas—she had never been able to resist. So, after dinner when she felt him come up behind her, as she stood at the kitchen sink, arranging the dishes in the soapy dishwater, her stomach fluttered in lustful anticipation. He immersed his hands in the warm water, clasping them over hers. He began gently massaging them while grazing the length of her tilted neck with the tip of his tongue. Bringing his body closer to hers, she could feel his erection through his pants. *Damn, that feels good,* she thought to herself, as she unconsciously, but wantonly, pressed her behind closer to his hardness.

Thomas continued sensually, massaging her hands underneath the water, kissing her neck. His kisses soon trailed from the side of her neck to the front, as he forced her around to face him. Then their eyes met. "I've been waiting on you for so long baby," he said, panting in a husky whisper just before covering her mouth anxiously with his. Instinctively, Lydia received him with equal hunger.

What the hell are you doing? Lydia asked herself. She knew she'd been missing this kind of passion. Thomas was definitely making up for what she'd been missing as he continued pleasuring her with two of his fingers, massaging the inside of her thighs with his free hand, all the while tantalizing her with passion-filled kisses. Within minutes, she released her pleasure all over his hand.

"Mmm," Thomas groaned, all too proud of his accomplishment. He freed her lips from his, smiling seductively. "This is only the beginning, baby." He led her through her own house with strange familiarity. In the bedroom, he positioned her on the bed just the way he wanted her, then he disappeared, leaving her bewildered and throbbing for what she knew all too well awaited her. When he reentered the room, in one hand he had what looked like the remote control to her CD player, and in the other, a bowl of strawberries. He set the player where he wanted it, then put the remote on the nightstand and joined Lydia on the bed.

A reflective grin crossed his lips as the familiar music from R & B singer and songwriter Brian McKnight's debut CD began playing. Making love to slow jams had been a ritual between them. Maybe it is more fitting to say, one of their rituals. Thomas had always been a romantic and attentive lover. So she could only imagine what was getting ready to go down with the strawberries being brought into the mix.

Lydia smiled as Thomas slid her body so that her head was just below the headboard. Her body shivered with delightful, nervous anticipation as Thomas slid her skirt and panties down her legs. On his way back up, he teased her inner thighs with the warmth and wetness of his tongue. When he found the center of her desire, she instinctively, palmed the back of his smooth head. Flicking her clitoris masterfully with the tip of his tongue, Thomas had Lydia almost screaming, sending her body into convulsive-like movements across every inch of the bed.

"Okay, okay Thomas," Lydia pleaded. "I can't take it anymore," she cooed, grabbing the thickness of his erection. "Please..." she pleaded again.

"No, not yet," Thomas denied her as be began dipping one strawberry at a time in and out of her center. She'd almost forgotten how big Thomas was on foreplay. He received no further interruption from her. By the time he'd finished, Lydia had cum multiple times and could hardly contain herself. Breathing heavily from the pleasure she'd just received, Lydia reached inside her side drawer, retrieving a condom from the supply she kept just in case. As spontaneous as her behavior was tonight, she wasn't so far gone not to make sure they were safe. She'd already suffered the consequence of making that mistake before.

Safety precautions taken care of, Thomas aligned his body with hers, teasing her by dipping the head of his hardness, quickly in and out of her, just enough to make her pull him into her. As he stroked her long and gently, he stretched his hands towards her head, sliding his fingers through her hair. He knew she liked that. Thomas knew and did everything, and then some, just the way he knew she liked it. This night was all about her pleasure.

When Thomas quickened the pace of his stroke, she could tell he was about to climax. He grabbed her hair tighter and pulled her closer to him. She pressed the tips of her fingers into his back dripping with perspiration, preparing for her own climax. Their eyes locked as they simultaneously reached their pleasure peaks.

The next time Lydia opened her eyes, the clock read 4:30 A.M, an hour and a half before she had to get up for work. She had the weirdest dream about a wild night of sex with Thomas. But, she soon realized it wasn't a dream when she felt Thomas' limp body still on top of hers, his soft penis still partially inside her. She rolled her eyes to the top of her head. *So much for taking it slow,"* she thought pitifully to herself.

Last night was fantastic, Lydia reluctantly admitted to herself. Fantastic, but wrong. Sex had always been like that between them. This time, though, unlike the other times, something wasn't sitting right with her. It was dawning on her at that very moment that maybe all of this time she had been thinking that there was this great, undying love between them when all there was, was really great sex! Other than sex, was there anything else?

Lydia slowly and carefully wiggled her body from beneath Thomas. She covered her naked body in her baby doll blue Victoria's Secret signature robe before going to the kitchen to start some coffee. Her head was pounding. She needed to take something before it got worse. Hurrying to the bathroom, she searched the medicine cabinet. When she located the lone bottle of Tylenol, she dumped the last two pills in her hand. She swallowed them with some water from the bathroom sink. Opening the bathroom door, she nearly bumped into Thomas.

"Shit, Thomas!"

A naughty smile spread across his lips. "Didn't mean to scare you," Thomas said, taking her hand. "It's kind of early. You couldn't sleep?"

Without responding, she led him back to the bedroom. Inside, Thomas covered his bottom half with the covers as he rested his back on the headboard. Quietly, Lydia was glad, because she was getting excited again at the sight of his naked body. Um, um, um. The loud screeching of the coffee pot interrupted her naughty thoughts. "Oh, the coffee," Lydia said, standing up, getting ready to go to the kitchen. But Thomas stopped her.

"No. You stay here. I'll get it." *There he goes again, exposing that body*, Lydia thought to herself, as Thomas exited the room stark naked. A few minutes later he returned carrying a tray with two coffee mugs, creamer, and sugar. Lydia tried to help him, but Thomas wouldn't have it. He was insistent on handling everything. He was a little sloppy, spilling some coffee on her nightstand, but he was doing his best. It was kind of cute.

The two of them sipped their coffee in comfortable silence as Lydia thought of how the previous night was not a part of her plan, while Thomas thought of how happy he was that they finally connected again. They sat on each side of the bed for several minutes before Thomas finally spoke. "I take it you're not feeling too good about what happened last night, huh?" he asked.

Lydia paused before answering, wanting to say the right words. But what would they be? She couldn't quite put into words what she was feeling. "Honestly, I don't really know how I feel," she stammered. "The only thing I do know is that this wasn't supposed to happen so soon, if at all."

"Lydia, you can't fight instinct. And that's exactly what happened last night," Thomas responded confidently. "You can't plan things when they're real—they just happen. Nothing can interfere with fate." Thomas turned towards her and began rubbing her shoulders. "I know things haven't been perfect between us—and that was my fault, I know. But I'm ready to do the right thing now." He turned her face to his, penetrating her eyes. "Lydia, you're what's good for me—always have been."

A familiar reaction stirred within Lydia. Her heart leaped, while her stomach did somersaults. She hated that Thomas always had this affect on her, no matter how badly he had treated her.

Here it was, after all this time, he was confessing that *she* was good for him. Just because she was good for him didn't mean that *he* was good for her. Men were slow learners, she knew. But she didn't have to keep putting her heart on the line to be trampled on. She didn't know where last night was going to lead.

What she did know was that it wasn't going to lead to another broken heart for her.

Later that evening, Lydia was having dinner with Sandra, Kania, Vanessa, and a woman named Lisa. Vanessa was Kania's wild, troublesome younger sister. Lisa was Kania's friend from law school. They were at Ramondo's, a popular Italian restaurant downtown Royal Oak, a suburb of Detroit, which featured a local jazz band every week.

It was an unofficial bridal party meeting to get started with the plans for Kania's approaching December wedding, a little less than six months away. As this would be the first wedding Lydia ever participated in, she had no idea what to expect. But she was definitely excited about the important role she would play. Although six months wasn't a lot of time to plan such an important event, she was sure that with Kania's tenacity for planning and keen eye for detail, the wedding would be a memorable event for all involved.

Kania was telling them about all the wedding consultants she'd been interviewing just as the waiter approached their table with their orders. The young attractive Mexican man, with the waviest hair Lydia had seen, moved quickly and efficiently. He disappeared just as quickly as he had arrived. When he was gone, everyone returned their attention to Kania who was ready to discuss bridal party duties.

"Lydia, you know you're going to be my Maid of Honor," she announced, smiling widely.

Accepting graciously, Lydia couldn't help noticing everyone trying to avoid looking in Vanessa's direction to judge her reaction. Vanessa would be the only one surprised by Kania's desire.

The two sisters had never gotten along, primarily because of Vanessa's jealousy toward Kania's success in her education, career, and now love. Vanessa was one of those women who didn't get along with most women, for one frivolous reason or another. Although a very pretty woman, with her smooth bronze skin, model-like high cheekbones, and big brown eyes, it all went to hell as soon as she opened her mouth. The girl was pure ghetto! And she cursed like a sailor for no good reason. There was no class, sophistication, or beauty about her, which is why she was usually the booty call girl with guys she thought she was in relationships with.

Before Lydia had started dating Roy a few years back, she and Vanessa had gotten into it over a man named Jeff, who had been dating both of them. When Jeff came to pick Lydia up, for what would turn out to be their last date, Vanessa, who'd followed him, rolled her car up on the curb of Lydia's neighbor's house, jumped out and ran wilding toward Lydia in attack mode. While she was accusing Lydia of fucking her man, Jeff yelled boldly and quite disrespectfully at her that she was just a part-time piece of ass to him. Still Vanessa focused her verbal and attempted physical attack on Lydia until, one of Lydia's neighbors called the police.

Even though she was pissed as hell at the scene Vanessa had caused in her otherwise quiet neighborhood, Lydia was embarrassed for Vanessa. Trying to be the bigger woman, Lydia had even gone to Vanessa to apologize for what happened, although she had played no part in Jeff's deception. But, Vanessa, like many women do, continued to take her anger out on Lydia.

From that moment on, Vanessa always had dagger eyes, through a forced smile, whenever she and Lydia crossed paths. She was only cordial in instances like this—when she had to be. Kania went on to her bridesmaids, which would be Vanessa, and a few of her cousins.

The only thing Lydia didn't like was that Kania wanted the bridal shower to be at Vanessa's apartment clubhouse, which meant that she and Vanessa would have more dealings with each other than either of them wanted. "Only for my girlfriend," Lydia reminded herself, while Sandra pretended to sulk at her inability to be in the wedding party because she'd be in the last trimester of her pregnancy, fully blown up. But Kania assured her that she wouldn't be left out in the least.

The official matters having been discussed, Kania started telling them some of the interesting details involved in the case she was working on. Sometimes when Lydia listened to all of the interesting and different situations Kania encountered in her line of work, she wondered if she should have pursued a career in civil law like Kania had encouraged her to when they were entering their second year in college. Kania never appeared bored with her work. Lydia only hoped that a promotion into the senior manager position would put an end to the monotony of her current position. If not, she just might have to consider a change in careers. If not law, possibly real estate. From what she'd been hearing, the field was working wonders for a lot of people she knew who were doing it on a part time basis.

Thinking of real estate turned Lydia's thoughts to Thomas. Successful real estate investing is what finally gave Thomas his way out of the military. He'd made some real estate contacts in a few of the different cities he'd lived in. And, so far, Thomas had purchased rental properties in Texas, Florida, and Atlanta, which had produced a pretty steady income.

When Lydia refocused on the present company, Vanessa had taken over the conversation, divulging entirely too much information for Lydia's taste about some wild sexual adventure she had had the previous weekend with a set of twins. While the others leaned in closer, not wanting to miss any of the juicy details, Lydia thought about the previous night that she'd spent sexing it up with Thomas and the day they'd spent together after he convinced her to skip out on work.

For the better part of the day, Thomas tried to convince Lydia that getting back with him was the best thing for her. Then something monumental occurred that was a first between her and Thomas—an argument. Thomas was describing the great life he would provide for Lydia, saying that with the money he was bringing in with his real estate ventures, she wouldn't have to be bothered with working. He'd be more than happy taking care of her, he claimed. All she would have to do was take care of the house and their children. But Lydia didn't see any nobility in his offer. To her, it seemed more like a strategic move to gain control over her.

That was exactly how her mother had gotten duped by her father, by placing all of her chips in one basket—his. When he up and deserted them, her mother realized that she didn't have a Plan B. So she always raised Lydia to be smarter than that.

"Oh, you can keep that offer," Lydia snapped. "I did not put myself through college with student loans, which I'm still paying for by the way, just so I could sit back and depend on some man to take care of me like *he* thinks I should be taken care of."

"What's so wrong with that?" Thomas asked clearly dumfounded.

"What's wrong with that?" Lydia asked mockingly. "No man can take care of me better that I can take care of myself. I've never set out to be anybody's kept woman."

"There you go getting all black womanish on me. And for what? Because a man has the audacity to want to fulfill his manly obligations as a provider?" Thomas said, seething.

"*Black womanish!*" Lydia's nostrils were flaring, she was so mad. Then she flipped him off with her hand. "Whatever the hell that means! Your pathetic offer has nothing to do with providing, but more to do with controlling. And I'm too independent for that shit," she added conclusively.

Thomas got her drift. "Okay, Lydia," he began softly. "We're getting ahead of ourselves here. The last thing I want to do is spend our day together arguing."

"Oh, so now you control when our argument is over?" Lydia spat.

A laugh slipped from his lips. "You've gotten quite feisty since I saw you last." He snuggled close to her from behind. "But I think it's sexy." He kissed her softly on the neck, softening her a little. He was right, though. They didn't need to spend the day arguing. But the truth of the matter was that Thomas didn't know how to handle arguing with Lydia, because he'd never encountered the argumentative side of her. In their past, Lydia had always made sure she kept her opinions to herself if they weren't in agreement with his. 'Okay, Thomas.' 'You're right, Thomas,' She wasn't that woman anymore.

No matter how hard he tried, Thomas was unsuccessful in improving the mood of their day. After a tasty breakfast, they took a walk along a scenic trail near Lydia's neighborhood, but they shared few words. Within a couple of hours, they were back at Lydia's house having more fantastic sex. But when Lydia awoke shortly after noon alone in her bed, she didn't know what to think.

"Are you listening?" Sandra shrieked with annoyance, bringing Lydia back to present company.

"I'm sorry. My mind trailed off to something that happened at work today," Lydia lied.

Sandra's response almost knocked the breath out of her. "If you were at work today, you'd better check with your in-charge office, because they told me you called off when I came there to meet you for lunch, like we'd planned."

Oh, shit! Lydia had completely forgotten about the lunch date. Usually Sandra called her when she was on the way, but Lydia dared not ask, not wanting to risk making herself look guilty. She knew better than to expect things to work in her favor when she was sneaking around with everyone's least favorite person.

"Oh, yeah," Sandra continued before Lydia could explain. "And what the hell were all those rose pedals all over your damn lawn? You must have had some romantic night and you're holding back on details." Suddenly all eyes were on her, looking for answers.

Sandra had probably driven to her house earlier when she'd discovered Lydia wasn't at work. If Lydia didn't say something quick, Sandra was going to get even busier with her inquiries. Well, the truth was definitely not an option. What would she say? 'Oh, I was just sleeping with Thomas. You know the man who all but left me at the altar? You know the one, right?'

Lydia began stammering. "Uhh, uhh, uhh. I…"

But Sandra cut her off. "Don't worry about it, girl. I know my cousin wasn't going to let you go that easy."

The mystery was solved, or so they all thought, thanks to Sandra. They finished eating their food over small talk. Lydia was just glad she didn't have to come up with a lie. She'd done enough of that already.

ELEVEN

Thomas was not surprised at all when his cell phone began to ring shortly after he and Lydia had made love and she had fallen asleep. The only surprise was that the calls hadn't started earlier. It had not been a part of his original plan to spend the night with Lydia, though he had no regrets. His marriage was a farce, but nonetheless, he was still married, and therefore, had to act accordingly. At least, to some degree.

He grimaced when he thought about his wife and how she had used his strong obligations of fatherhood to force him into marriage. Yes, that's exactly what happened, no matter what anyone else thought. Of course, Thomas was aware that he had operated under free will, but his wife was guilty of using deceitful tactics to push him in the direction that she wanted him to go.

They had only been dating—okay, fucking—for a few months. But when he met Lydia at that party, all that began to change. Immediately, his heart began going in Lydia's direction. Sensing that someone was taking the man she had claimed as her own, his wife, who'd told him in the beginning that she was on birth control, became pregnant, she knew that Thomas would never neglect his child as his father had done him. Maliciously, she threatened that if he didn't marry her and stay away from Lydia, she'd disappear, and make sure his child didn't know anything about him. She never admitted how she knew about Lydia, but the coldness in her once alluring green eyes made it clear that she had every intention of following through on her threat if he didn't follow suit.

Those same hard, cold eyes were the eyes he had awakened to for the last seven years. How could she be happy like this? Being with a man she knew didn't love her? He'd spent the first few years of their marriage trying to figure that out. After a few more years, he finally realized that it wasn't happiness she cared about, but control. Seemingly, she got off knowing that she had him by the balls, having the one thing that no other woman had—Thomas Jr. —whom he swore would never know the hurt and devastation of an absent, uncaring father.

He brought his car to a slower speed, decelerating a little at a time the closer he came to the exit that would lead him home. Thomas never thought a time would come that he'd really consider leaving Lena. Not for good, at least. The two things that had kept him afloat all these years—Thomas Jr. and sex—were no longer enough.

Sexually speaking, Thomas had what most men would die for—a wife who allowed him to sleep with other women, as long as she was around, sometimes as a participant. Talk about Heaven! Thomas took full advantage of this privilege every moment he could. And of course, he made a point to do it behind Lena's back, too. It was only during those times that the little setup was enjoyable.

But of all the women he slept with, though, his mind was never far from the one woman his soul craved. His heart's true desire was the one woman Lena warned him to stay away from—Lydia.

The very first time he made love to Lydia, when he knew that she'd chosen him to be her first, he knew she was as special to him as he was to her. She was so beautiful and enticing, yet just as angelic and demure. Lydia was not like the usual women he'd been with. Not at all. She had class. Sophistication. She was the epitome of a true lady, like no woman he'd known before, especially his own prostituting, drug-addicted mother. He was awestruck from the beginning.

Lena immediately became a thing of the past when Lydia came into his life. The wild, exotic sex she was giving him couldn't hold a candle to what was growing between him and Lydia. His attachment to Lydia was so strong that when Lena threatened him to stay away, secretly he cried; it was so hard to comply. He couldn't even come up with anything reasonably sensible to break things off with Lydia. Instead, he took the punk way out, saying and doing nothing at all.

So many times during Lena's pregnancy, he regretfully admitted that he'd hoped she'd fall down a flight of steps or something. Anything to make his mistake go away. But for the love of his unborn son, he pushed his own anger and unhappiness behind him and focused on the joy he hoped his son would bring into his life.

Joy is exactly what Thomas Jr. was from the moment he was born. For a while, Thomas did find happiness in his marriage when the focus was on him and Lena being good parents to their son. Then, about five years ago, his mind began wandering to the short-lived relationship that had blossomed with Lydia. Dangerously, he allowed his mind to imagine the "what-ifs" and the "what could've beens."

He envisioned the romantic night he would have planned asking Lydia to be his wife, how he'd whisk her away to someplace like the Pocono's or Niagara Falls, make love to her for hours, surprising her in the evening over dinner with the engagement ring he would've known was perfect for her. Further, his imagination allowed him to have clear sight of Lydia in her princess style wedding gown walking down the aisle as excited about their future as he was. They'd have two children, a boy and a girl. Not even the best fairytale could have had a happier ending.

Lydia wouldn't have been anything close to the nightmare of a wife that Lena had been. She was always trying to break down his sense of manhood. Starting arguments about nothing. Anything to get him fired up, keeping him under her control. Quite the opposite, Lydia would have been welcoming him home every night with loving, open arms if she had been afforded the kind of life Lena had. She would have allowed him to be the head of their household, having the final say on all major issues. Loving him just that much, Lydia wouldn't have felt any less of a woman standing slightly behind her man, where she belonged.

Soon enough Thomas' imagination got the best of him and was no longer enough to satisfy him. His fantasies of what life would've been like with Lydia were far too tortuous for him to endure. Finally, after encountering so many men who managed to maintain relationships with their children through divorce or out-of-wedlock pregnancies, Thomas realized that he could, too. This wasn't the day and age where people denied their heart's desire for the sake of the children. Truth be told, some children were even better off when their parents broke up.

More hopeful than he'd been since that fateful day when he said, "I do," Thomas made a decision to follow his heart back to Lydia. When he was promoted to a second level recruiter for the army, he lucked out on the opportunity to travel. That's when his plan really began to formulate. Since he had to travel to different cities, sometimes for a week or two at a time, Lena couldn't keep track of his whereabouts as she had been accustomed to doing, so Thomas made the most of his good fortune.

The first thing he did was to use his contacts at MSU's alumni association to verify that Lydia was still in the Michigan area. He wasn't surprised that she was, remembering how close she and her mother were. That was something he liked teasing her about.

The first time he was near Michigan for business, the first item on his personal agenda was to connect with Lydia. Using a bogus explanation about being shipped off to Cuba, he began his search. He found her in the same apartment he had helped her find after college.

A range of emotions engulfed them at first sight. It was visibly deep in her eyes—astonishment, hurt, anger, happiness. In the end, he managed to convince her with his story. Thomas couldn't have been happier, even knowing that the most time he could give her was about three weeks. But it was the best three weeks he'd had in years, and it further convinced him that he belonged with Lydia.

It was hell on him to do it, but he had to leave her again. He knew she'd be hurt—again—but he swore to himself, he'd make her understand later that it was for the best.

When he could no longer put it off, Thomas sadly pulled into the driveway of the beautiful two-story townhouse he was renting. He felt sad that something so beautiful on the outside could be filled with such animosity, regret, and malice on the inside. He knew that this time would come eventually, so inhaling deeply, slowly turning the doorknob, he prepared himself to combat what was awaiting him inside.

It was quiet inside as usual for this time of day. Even though she wasn't working anywhere yet, Lena insisted on placing Thomas Jr. in daycare under the premise of finding employment, though Thomas knew that more of her time was spent trying to keep track of him.

Lena's venom filled the room when she finally appeared. Her heavily shadowed eyes met his and held them a few seconds before she fired at him, deliberating each word with a calculated edge. "Do you think I'm some kind of fool, Thomas?" She didn't wait for a response. "Don't think for one moment that I don't know what you've been up to with that little tramp you've been trying to get back with. I'm letting you know *right* now that I'm not having this shit!"

Closing the small space that was between them, standing inches from him, Lena raised her forefinger towards his face. "I advise you to think about your son before you go making some decisions you *think* you're man enough to handle because, like I've always told you, if you go against me, I swear, your son will only know the worst about you."

Lena was as predictable as rain in a thunderstorm. Thomas was the one who was finally changing in this game they'd been playing all these years. She pushed just the button he needed to set him off in a way she'd never seen before.

Before he knew it, his hand had seized the entirety of her neck, pushing her hard and suddenly against the wall. The thud of her small frame against the wall echoed in the silence of the room. "You *bitch!* I've had enough of you and your threats against my son. As a matter of fact, I've had enough of you!" If it wasn't for his son, he would have choked the life out of her, he hated her so much. "You can't control me anymore, Lena. You know full well where my heart lies. That may not matter to you, but it matters to me. You might as well know that I intend to go in the direction of my heart. And there's not a *damn* thing you can do about it!"

Finally he released her from his grip. She crumpled to the floor, grabbing her neck desperately in search of air. She was more shocked than scared. Throughout all of her disrespectful, controlling, and demeaning ways toward Thomas, this was the first time he'd ever stood up to her, let alone gotten physical with her. But she would be damned if she'd give him the satisfaction of seeing that he rattled her.

Gathering herself as best she could, Lena stood to her feet and searched for her voice. "I knew you were a fool, Thomas, the first time I saw you. But I had given you credit, at least, for knowing me a little better than you obviously do." Having picked herself off the floor, she regained her composure, taking long, confident strides towards him, intimidatingly circling him. "I hope you don't think I would come to the city where my husband's ex-girlfriend lives and not find out all that I need to know about her." A threatening laugh escaped her lips. "If you think you love this Lydia so much, you might do her a world of good by staying away from her—before some unforeseen accident occurs, perhaps in the parking lot of Global-Tel. We'll see how tough you'll be then."

Strategically, Lena made sure she wasn't within arm's length of Thomas when she made her little threat. Thomas was quick to respond. "If one hair on her head is harmed, Lena, I swear, you'll wish I had choked you to death a few minutes ago."

Lena smiled thinly. "Try me if you want to, Thomas."

TWELVE

A fter almost four hours inside Cobo Convention Center downtown, Lydia was pooped. She and Kania had been at a bridal show. It was a first for both of them. Of course, Kania, was much more excited than Lydia about the entire affair. Yes, the fashion extravaganza was exciting, showcasing every designer wedding gown one could imagine, from traditional, to exotic, to contemporary, not to mention bridesmaids' dresses and tuxedos of varying styles. But the ridiculously long lines at the practically unquantifiable number of vendor tables were just absurd. From floral vendors, to jewelry vendors, to cake vendors, to stationary vendors. It was absolutely exhausting.

Lydia had never been a part of the planning stages of a wedding. So she had no idea there would be so much to it. If she hadn't had so much going on in her personal life, she probably would've been more excited about the process. But after the ten and twelve-hour days she'd been working the past couple of weeks, Kania's wedding was the last thing she wanted to think about.

God, she couldn't wait for the new senior manager to be selected. It seemed like until that time, she, along with Angela and Stanley, were like slaves to the company, having to be available whenever called upon, even outside of work hours. They had to prove they could be depended upon and prove that they were senior manager material.

Unfortunately, her competition, Angela and Stanley, didn't quite grasp this concept as well as she did. Both of them had called off more than once, a few times on the same day, leaving Lydia to cover their teams as well as her own. Lydia had to sit through two and three-hour conference calls about items that could've been covered in an E-mail. She also had to evaluate over fifty service representatives on their call handling skills and conduct team meetings. The days had been ridiculously busy. But Lydia didn't mind showing that *she* could handle it.

Of course, that didn't leave any time for much else. That included her mother, who'd called her three times this week, or Sandra, who had called more than that. Lydia couldn't even fit time in for the gym. And, no matter how hard he tried to change it, Lydia didn't have any time for Thomas either.

Between her cell phone, home phone, and work phone, she'd lost count of how many messages he'd left for her. Two days of his over-persistence was pissing Lydia off. Thomas had crossed the line of flattery into the dark territory of aggravation and pure inconsideration for her job with his popup visits at her office and home.

What kind of person does that? He was behaving rudely and childishly, as though neither one of them had responsibilities outside of each other. Lydia had no problem respecting when he couldn't talk to her at various times during the day when he was in meetings and what not. However, she really had no choice because he simply didn't answer his phone.

She could only imagine what either Sandra or Kania would say, *if* she were able to talk to them about it. But that was out of the question.

"Hmph, screen your calls. Let his calls go straight to voicemail," Kania would say. "Just shake that monkey off your back," Sandra might well offer. Even though girlfriend advice could cause more harm than good in some situations, most times it could be just what the doctor ordered.

The closest she got to shaking Thomas off her back for awhile was to promise to see him. The only problem was, she hadn't anticipated such an exhausting time at the bridal show. But she knew there could be no backing out with Thomas now, so her best bet was to hurry up the rest of her time with Kania so she could possibly get a nap in or something before Thomas came over.

Summer had about two more weeks of life remaining, at least, according to the calendar, which didn't carry much weight in Michigan. Cold temperatures could swoop down on them in a moment's notice. But today the weather was nice, an even 70 degrees.

Lydia and Kania were dressed coolly in lightweight pants suits. A nice breeze was blowing as they walked to where the car was parked on one of the side streets near the convention center. Kania spent the five-minute walk rehashing almost every thrilling detail of the show, excitedly trying to bounce off ideas she wanted to incorporate into her wedding on a half-listening Lydia. When Kania realized Lydia's attention was elsewhere, she frowned.

"I'll only excuse you for ignoring me if you tell me you were thinking about Roy and the rose pedal night," she said, smiling.

Lydia responded with a smile, allowing Kania to think that was the case. She couldn't be accused of lying about the ordeal when she'd never opened her mouth, right? On the ride home, Lydia gave Kania her fullest attention, ensuring there was no more talk of Roy and rose pedals.

"Uhm…yes, Ma…I…uhhh…got your message," Lydia finally managed to say as she unsuccessfully pushed Thomas away from her neck. They were nestled in her bed together the next morning, following their steamy night of lovemaking. Thomas continued pleasuring her underneath the covers, which would have been erotic in a naughty kind of way, had the caller not been her mother.

Caroline was fussing at Lydia for letting her work commitments distract her to the point that she had not so much as dropped by her house in over a week, let alone returned her calls. She'd called Lydia quite a few times over the past week and Lydia had not returned a single one of them. Knowing that she was completely wrong, Lydia felt awful. And she knew that it wasn't work, alone, that was distracting her. Thomas was, too.

Lydia had tried blowing him off. But he was beyond persistent. He refused to take no for an answer. Either he'd be waiting for her at her car when she got off work or waiting in her driveway when she got home. Lydia was too tired from work to do much away from the house. But Thomas was more than willing to relax her with his insatiableness in the bedroom.

"What if there had been some sort of emergency or something?" Caroline was saying. "Don't bother with apologies either. Just don't let it happen again."

Though she felt a twinge of guilt, Lydia still didn't appreciate being chastised by her mother as though she were a child. So while Caroline continued fussing, Lydia allowed herself to revel in the soft wetness of Thomas' lips against the skin of her inner thigh and her center of passion.

Lydia knew she was beside herself. The rational side of her mind told her that the great sex she was having with Thomas was distracting her from the important issues between them. But the sensual side was enjoying the distraction.

She was so lost in the moment that a small moan escaped her lips as Thomas plunged two of his fingers inside her.

"*What in the…?*" Caroline screeched! "I *know* you're not doing what it sounds like you're doing."

"No, Ma! I'm not doing anything." Lydia tried to cover, but it was useless. *God, this was so embarrassing!* "Ma, I'm…" The click of the phone cut her off. Just like that the situation had gone from bad to worse. Lydia held the phone a few more minutes while the shock and humiliation encompassed her. Knowing there was nothing she could do, finally, she pressed the power button to turn the phone off.

Sitting back on the bed, Lydia couldn't help but notice the grin across Thomas' face. "This is funny to you, huh?" Lydia asked angrily, her tone sharp.

"What?" He was mocking her.

"Don't act like you don't know what I'm talking about You should have cut that shit out once you knew I was talking to my mother," she barked. Lydia began furiously sifting through the pile of clothes on the floor that had accumulated over the past week. Having located her robe, she put it on, tying it tightly around her waist.

"Hold up," Thomas began, his voice calm, but serious. "I didn't hear any objections from you a few minutes ago when that big grin was across your face." He stood up from the bed stark naked, holding her gaze steady. "You wouldn't be having this problem if you'd grow the hell up and stop letting everybody run your life. It shouldn't be a secret that we're seeing each other again. To hell with what they have to say about it." He added, with a smirk, "I thought you'd grown out of this momma's girl routine by now."

Lydia was stunned silent. *Momma's girl?* The nerve of him—trying to make her feel like a kid because she still had a close relationship with her mother. It shouldn't have surprised her though, seeing that he had always been jealous of the closeness between her and her mother. It went back to when they had first begun dating. He started by making small jokes about how often she and her mother spoke on the phone. He would try to make her feel guilty about visiting her mother on weekends, claiming he missed her so much. Lydia told herself it was nothing to take too seriously, but still she stopped mentioning her mother to Thomas as much.

Thomas was doing the same thing now that he did back then. Trying to take up all of her free time, keeping her from her family and friends. Lydia didn't know any better back then. Being a sucker for love was her excuse for falling for his antics. But things had changed since then. *She* had changed.

"Fuck you, Thomas!" Lydia snapped ferociously. "Why in the hell would I want to broadcast from the mountain tops that I'm fucking around again with the same asshole who only treats me like shit every opportunity I give him!" Lydia huffed, allowing her anger to fill every word. "Of course you don't care if everybody knows about us because when it's all over, you're nowhere to be found and I'm left cleaning up the mess!"

No sooner than the last word left from her mouth, Thomas was at her feet, his arms wrapped around her waist. He was holding her for dear life. His grip was so tight, she momentarily lost her breath. Shock registered across his face like he'd just been caught with his pants around his ankles. "What the hell is the problem, Lydia? I'm trying to fix things between us."

Lydia was exasperated, filled with confusion. "What exactly are you trying to fix between us, Thomas—sex—because that seems to be the *only* thing that works for us?"

Thomas stared blankly at her like she had two heads attached to her shoulders. "What's that supposed to mean, Lydia? You're talking like there's no hope." He sounded defeated as he slumped onto the floor.

"And you're talking like I don't have reason to," Lydia fired back with an edginess that Thomas was reluctantly getting used to.

"I can't do this by myself, Lydia. If that's how you feel, what have we been doing over these past few weeks?" Thomas asked.

"That's exactly what I've been wondering lately," Lydia said honestly, not as harsh. "We've been down this road before. The only difference is that I'm not as naïve and foolishly in love as before."

Thomas stood up and began gathering his things, getting dressed. He was somber, clearly disappointed, and feeling more hopeless than he ever thought he would be about where Lydia's head was in regard to them. "I knew I had some making up to do, but I always thought we were on the same page about what we wanted. Obviously, I was mistaken."

"Obviously," Lydia replied icily.

Lydia watched him take his time gathering his things, like he was waiting for her to say something comforting to him. Pitiful. That time had passed. She was no longer consumed with how Thomas felt. She'd traveled that rocky road long enough. She was sick and tired of it.

In years past Lydia had gone out of her way to avoid hurting Thomas, even going against her own feelings and better judgment. Thanks to Thomas, Lydia stared the hard knocks of love eye-to-eye. It wasn't pretty. But as her mother said time and time again, having your heart broken is just a part of living.

It was an unavoidable part of growing up.

Another part of growing up was learning to let go of the past, the good and the bad. When it came to Thomas, for some reason, Lydia couldn't seem to grasp that concept. Until now. It was dawning on her that maybe there was a simple reason he'd chosen to ignore why things had never worked for them.

She thought of these things and more as she watched him waiting for her to ease his pain and tell him that they had a possibility of a future. For the first time, Lydia was far from sure of that.

The room stood still as the uncertainty between them took over. Silence crowded the room for what felt like much longer than the actual few minutes that it was, until a loud shattering of glass coming from the front of the house startled them both.

Lydia jumped up first, tightening the belt around her robe, getting ready to run towards the noise until Thomas held her back.

Irritatingly, he frowned. "You stay here," he commanded.

Reluctantly, she did as he told her, relieved that she wasn't alone. Fright rippled through her as already broken pieces of glass were crushed more under the weight of Thomas' feet as he looked around for a possible break in or something. Tons of things floated through Lydia's mind while Thomas was investigating. One in particular was that someone had tried to break into her house while not one, but two cars were in the driveway. She couldn't believe this was happening!

Now she was no expert, but she knew there was a more inconspicuous method to breaking into a house besides shattering a window. Could it have been something personal—possibly related to the hang-up calls she'd been receiving? Her intuition was telling her this wasn't just a random act of violence that Thomas was trying to sell her.

"It happens all the time, especially in crime-ridden cities like Detroit," he explained knowingly. "The little glimpse I was able to get of the car speeding off, it looked like some kids were inside. Probably teenagers. More than likely, they got your house by accident. You know your porch light isn't on."

She wanted him to be right. That would be a hell of a lot easier to swallow than her being personally targeted for reasons she was oblivious to. She picked up the phone by her bed to call the police. Thomas flipped! "Don't put yourself through that nonsense. Like I said, it was probably just some silly teenagers. Believe me, it'll be more trouble than it's worth reporting it to the police. I'll make sure your window is fixed by the time you get off work tomorrow."

Lydia agreed to drop it. Before he left, Thomas found some boxes in her basement and hoisted them up to cover the medium-sized hole in her window. He made sure that she was sound asleep before he snuck out of the bed to his car.

The drive home was a tumultuous one for Thomas as he stressed over the mess he'd made of things.

Focusing intensely on the road before him, Thomas struggled to stay within the confines of his lanes on the freeway. He drove under the speed limit, in no rush to get home. He needed time to think.

What he thought was an uncomplicated plan of sweeping Lydia off her feet again was turning into anything but that. This newfound attitude of hers was driving him nuts! At the same time that he was growing frustrated with her hesitation, he understood where she was coming from. He knew how women's minds, especially Lydia's, worked. She was probably thinking he was just full of games, that he was going to play with her feelings, get her hopes all high, then disappear on her again.

He'd been an asshole. It didn't take rocket science to figure that one out. He swore that if she'd just give him one last chance, he could make her understand. He needed that to happen sooner rather than later before his seemingly over the edge wife did something more than throw a rock through Lydia's window.

One day Thomas promised he'd be honest with Lydia about everything from their past. But he would never admit to the danger he brought her way through Lena's antics. No matter what, he would make sure Lena never got this close to Lydia again. Protecting Lydia was the only thing on his mind as he secretly removed the brick that was thrown through her window with the handwritten note attached to it threatening further danger if she saw Thomas again.

THIRTEEN

———————✠———————

Two weeks passed since the brick came crashing through Lydia's front window in the middle of the night. And just as he'd promised, Thomas had her window repaired by the time she got off work the following day. A white passenger-style van bearing the name of Roy's Home & Auto Glass Repair was steering away from her house as she turned the corner in the direction of her house. Too bad that Thomas couldn't do anything about the damn hang up calls, which had increased in frequency on both her cell and home phones over the past month. Since he couldn't, Lydia went against his advice of not involving the police.

As far as Lydia knew, the prank phone calls, and the broken window were related. She'd done everything she knew how to do—answer the calls, not answer the calls, challenge the caller to say something, anything. Nothing worked. Not even having the number changed temporarily, as recommended by the Annoyance Call Bureau of Global-Tel, who investigated matters like these. But no sooner had the two-week period expired and her phone numbers were returned back to normal, the calls resumed!

Once she confided in Sandra and Kania about the window incident, they all but dragged her to the police station to make the report.

"No way do you keep putting up with this shit!" Kania was furious. "People play these games not realizing there are serious consequences." Sandra wasn't as passionate, but she had similar sentiments.

Through connections she had with a friend who worked in the police department, Kania had a trace put on her phone. She put an interesting thought into Lydia's head that the prankster could be one of the competitors for the senior manager position at her job, trying to rattle her, and throw her off her game.

While neither Angela nor Stanley seemed the type to go to such extremes, it wasn't that farfetched. Competition in corporate America was ruthless, driving some people to extreme measures to move up that ladder of success. Lots of backstabbing. She wouldn't rule it out.

Kania met Lydia at the police station downtown to pick up the copy of the report. On the third floor they were greeted by a stern-faced, but still attractive, mahogany skinned, thirty-something officer, whose obvious muscular frame was fitted perfectly in his uniform. He introduced himself as Officer Boyle. Kania called him Chris. He was her inside connection and a childhood friend.

"Thanks a lot, Chris, for expediting this matter for my friend." Kania said to Officer Boyle, who, she noticed hadn't taken his eyes off Lydia. "We really want to get to the bottom of this as quickly as possible. It's already been going on for far too long." She added, shifting her blameful eyes towards Lydia, who turned to avoid her eyes.

"I know, I know. I should've already reported the harassment. It just seemed kind of silly at first." Lydia explained. Kania was still fussing when Officer Boyle interjected.

"It's nothing to get too worried about. Kania's always been a worry wart," he smiled at Kania. Then to Lydia he said, "We should know something in less than two weeks. So just sit tight, okay."

Lydia was comforted by Officer Boyle's words. He walked with them outside. Kania was parked closer to the building, so once she was in her car, Lydia was left alone with Officer Boyle. Slyly, he persuaded Lydia to talk a little more in depth about her perspective of what was going on while he walked her the extra block to her car.

"You say you haven't made any recent enemies that you know of, huh?" Lydia couldn't help noticing the perfect set of teeth in his mustache-framed mouth. It was rare to come across a man with such a beautiful set of teeth. *Good grooming habits*, Lydia noted. It was hard not to stare as she responded, without mentioning the part of getting back involved with Thomas.

"The only thing that comes to mind is that I and two of my coworkers are competing for a promotion. Truthfully, neither of them strikes me as the type to stoop to this level of intimidation. It has to be something random that's gotten out of hand," she said, sounding more like she was trying to convince herself.

"It is hard to imagine anyone wanting to harass someone as sweet as you." Officer Boyle was flirting with her! His professionalism returned when they reached her truck. "Like I said, we should have some answers for you real soon." He withdrew a business card from his left pocket, bearing the name C.B. Security, Owner, Chris Boyle. Handing it to her, he said, "If you need anything in the meantime, don't hesitate to call. Okay?"

What else could she say? "Okay. Thanks." Officer Boyle walked away, seemingly proud of his accomplishment of opening the door for further communication between himself and Lydia.

Almost a week later, driving north on the Lodge freeway to Sandra's house to accompany her to a doctor's appointment, Lydia was more than flattered with Officer Chris Boyle's subtle move on her. It kind of made her day. She had no immediate plans to call him, though. There was more than enough on her plate, between Roy and Thomas. But she'd keep his card handy for possible future use.

Lydia was still smiling when she pulled in the driveway of Sandra's Farmington Hills home until she noticed that Lester's car was in front of her. She hoped it didn't mean what it looked like. If she'd taken time out of her schedule to take this woman to her appointment and Sandra had decided to have Lester do it, she'd be too through! Lately, Sandra couldn't make a clear decision to save her life. One minute she didn't want Lester to have anything to do with her or the pregnancy. The next minute she'd be going off about him acting like he didn't care. Sometimes she'd go to her doctor appointments alone. Other times she'd demand that Lester take time out of his schedule and go with her. This time she couldn't decide what she wanted. The last Lydia heard was that she was supposed to be going with Sandra. So why the hell was Lester here?

When a furious Sandra came storming and wobbling out the front door, she got her answer. If Lester wasn't such an asshole, Lydia would probably feel sorry for the hell Sandra was giving him. She was sure he felt much like a ping-pong ball with the way Sandra's mood changed with him.

"Asshole," Sandra muttered under her breath when she pulled herself into Lydia's truck. Even angry, Sandra still managed to have that ever present pregnancy glow, stylishly dressed in DKNY maternity denim jeans and a white top bearing the word "baby" on the front with an arrow pointing down towards her belly.

Lydia didn't bother inquiring what the problem was because it could've been anything. As far as she was concerned, Sandra deserved much credit for dealing with her pregnancy, an illegitimate child from her unfaithful husband, and a six-year old daughter. To think, she hadn't killed anyone yet! It wasn't necessary for Lydia to pry for information. Sandra knew Lydia's ear would be open whenever she was ready.

Prenatal appointments seemed to be the best kinds of doctor's visits that existed. The objective being to make the expectant mother as comfortable as possible, the front desk attendants were usually friendlier and more eager to please than other such personnel in most hospitals Lydia had been to. Most others acted like your presence at the counter was an interruption to whatever they were doing.

There were paintings of pregnant women, infants, and smiling tots decorating the walls. When Lydia and Sandra entered the office, the ladies at the front desk immediately stopped their chatter and greeted them warmly. The friendly staff consisted of three female nurses, and one male nurse. Sandra was now at the point in her pregnancy where she was coming to the doctor every other week, so everyone knew her, not to mention that this was the same obstetrician/gynecologist that Sandra had when she was pregnant with Alicia. As things were ten times better between Sandra and Lester back then, Lydia hadn't gone to many of those appointments, but she'd been to enough this time around that the staff was pretty familiar with her, too.

There were two other mothers-to-be in the waiting room—one accompanied by a man, presumably her husband, the other by herself. Knowing that they'd have a bit of a wait until Sandra was called to the back, they each grabbed one of their choice magazines and settled in front of the wall mounted T.V., which was playing some health program.

"Mrs. Anderson, would you please step over to the desk for a moment?" a smiling robust, rosy cheeked nurse called to Sandra.

When Sandra waddled back to her seat, Lydia was awaiting the answer to the quiz question about what the leading cause of death was for African American women. Since the program was all about heart disease, Lydia wasn't surprised at all that her answer was correct. She was making a mental note to tell Denise that this was the type of programming she should subscribe to for viewing at her fitness center when Sandra broke into her thoughts.

Sandra's hair, which had long since grown out of the close-cropped cut she normally wore, had fallen from behind her ear, and was hanging over one eye. "You know you had me looking like a complete idiot, shooting my mouth off to Roy about the romantic gesture of sprinkling the rose pedals across your lawn. I can't believe you haven't told me who this new man is in your life." Her head was cocked to the side, awaiting Lydia's response.

"Mrs. Anderson," the nurse called from behind the door. "You can come in now."

Saved by the bell, Lydia breathed a sigh of relief. Before Sandra disappeared behind the door, she turned, warning Lydia, "Don't think I'm done with you, missy."

Lydia knew that Sandra wouldn't be long with the doctor. She had to come up with something fast and believable. Sometimes being close friends with someone made it next to impossible to lie to them, because they could see straight through you. At least that's the way it was with her and Sandra. That being the case, Lydia silently wished she could leave Sandra to fend for herself getting home. Of course, she couldn't.

Her mind continued churning. "Got it!" Lydia snapped her fingers, as her lie began to formulate in the last minutes she had before Sandra would be back in the lobby. There was a guy at work who'd shown mild interest in Lydia about a year before at her company picnic. He was a short, stubby little man, who was several inches shorter than Lydia. Lydia couldn't have been less interested. But he was attractive enough for Sandra to believe that Lydia had gone on one date with him. She inhaled deeply, trying to calm her nerves, so that it wouldn't be so obvious that the story had been concocted only minutes before.

Luckily for Lydia, though, when Sandra came out of the doctor's office, she had completely forgotten about the mystery man, and began gabbing about the baby, who they knew was a boy, had a strong heartbeat, good fetal growth, and such. That was all Sandra talked about from the time they left the doctor's office until they reached the restaurant where they had brunch.

When the topic of Lester was broached, the mood soured. Lydia listened as Sandra described her mixed emotions over the pregnancy that she had been waiting for, and how the excitement was dampened by the news that Lester had conceived a baby with another woman.

Sandra was flipping pieces of lettuce around in her salad bowl as she spoke quietly. "I've accepted so much from him, with his constant affairs and everything. You know, regardless of what anybody says, that's what marriage is—accepting some things even when they're not right. But, damn it, I, at least, expected him to protect me and our family from *this* kind of bullshit. I mean, a *baby!* What the hell was he thinking?" Lydia saw the tears forming in Sandra's eyes before one finally gave way and slid down her face.

She wished she could comfort her friend. Sandra's raw emotion made Lydia reminiscent of the devastation she'd felt when Thomas had deserted her. Now she could understand how helpless her family and friends felt. Lydia had to get through it on her own. Since this wasn't the first time for Sandra, she was more than familiar with the healing process. Now, the question was, did Sandra want to go through that process again, or try something different?

Rather than say anything, Lydia placed her hand comfortingly on top of Sandra's until she regained her composure. Over their main courses, Lydia described the details of the bridal show, embellishing the parts she really hadn't paid that much attention to. Then Sandra brought her up to speed on Alicia and the new private school she was attending.

On the drive home, Lydia frowned as she thought about what Roy must be thinking now that Sandra had opened her mouth about the flowers on her front lawn. Of course he'd conclude that he was right in his assumption that their breakup had everything to do with Thomas, which was only partially correct, but no one would believe or understand what was really going on.

Lydia appreciated that Roy wasn't callous enough to spill the beans to Sandra or her mother about Thomas. If he had wanted to wreak havoc on Lydia as payback, he certainly had a major piece of information. Thank God he wasn't that type of man.

So why was she casting him off for the likes of Thomas Cunningham, like Roy wasn't a man worth holding on to? Lydia sighed heavily, holding the steering wheel steady, remaining carefully in her own lane, when she noticed a car behind her driving way too close. Like she normally did when drivers behaved that way, Lydia intentionally kept her same speed. She was sure the driver would get the point and drive on around her.

Watching the driver behind her, Lydia resumed her thoughts. None of this was supposed to have happened. She hadn't planned to have to explain anything about Thomas to Roy, nor to have reignited the sexual pleasure between her and Thomas. The only good thing that had come from that was the realization that sex was, apparently, the only good thing between them.

It was a downright shame that it had taken getting into this mess to realize what everybody else already knew. Roy was a great catch!

Roy was an attractive man in his early thirties and was an entrepreneur at heart. He went to college to study International Business, but he learned during his four and a half years that his mild-mannered personality wasn't cutthroat enough to play the corporate game. So, he combined his business management skills and his love for automotives. With a well-constructed business plan, he applied for a small business loan from the bank, and with the money, he bought into an auto supply franchise. He was so successful that, within five years, he was successfully managing three stores in the metro Detroit area.

Roy wasn't interested in womanizing, though he definitely had the smooth mannerisms and confidence for it. Instead he treated most women as ladies, like he was raised to do. More importantly, Roy wanted a wife, not just another piece of ass. He'd been there and done that in his twenties. Now he was ready to get married, have a family, and build a life with the woman he loved. That woman was Lydia.

The thought resonated in her mind that she made a big mistake by breaking up with Roy, and it was too much to bear. Lydia found herself exiting the freeway in the direction of her favorite strip mall that contained a couple of her favorite shopping spots, TJ Maxx and DSW, a mega discount designer shoe store. These had always been her spots when she needed to relieve her mind of any kind of pressures. Emotional shopping, the experts called it. Well, Lydia rationalized that as long as she wasn't charging up credit cards, she was okay.

She started with DSW. It never took her long to find a sexy pair of pumps. Less than twenty minutes later she was dropping one pair of casual red pumps and one pair of slingback pumps into her trunk. Then she was off to T.J. Maxx, where she'd really do some major damage. It was no telling how many cute outfits she'd piece together.

Beginning in the front of the store, Lydia looked at the Jones New York career separates, then DKNY. After a few minutes she moved on, not being much in the mood for work clothes. Jeans, knit tops, and active wear was where her desires were. Clothes to just chill and relax in. She was making her way to the size six jeans when she heard her name being called. It wasn't coming from too far behind her, and it was getting closer, more familiar.

Surprised, she turned to see a smiling Angelina a few steps from her.

"Hey, girl!" Angelina smiled widely. She was dressed in a pair of dark blue Baby Phat jeans, with a matching jacket covering a basic white tee. Judging from the number of bags she was holding in both hands, either Angelina was having her own bout of emotional shopping or she was preparing her wardrobe for the coming Michigan fall and winter seasons.

"Hey!" Lydia returned. "Funny seeing you here. Looks like you've been here awhile, too."

Angelina nodded her head. "Yeah, I had some coats for me and my son in the layaway that I just took out. Plus, I picked up some more items. You know, I love shopping."

"I can tell," Lydia said. She prepared to walk away. "Don't let me keep you. Looks like you were on your way out."

"Only to put these bags in the car," Angelina replied quickly. "I've still got some things to look for. If you don't mind, why don't we finish up together?"

Lydia normally preferred shopping alone, but she didn't want to appear rude. Besides, Angelina was beginning to grow on her. "No problem," she said.

Angelina bounced away with her bags and returned in under five minutes. As they rounded the store's several racks of clothes, Angelina did most of the talking about her son and all the sports activities that she had to run him around to practice for or to play games. After listening to Angelina, Lydia no longer had any pity for Sandra, who only had to take Alicia to a dance class once a week and Girl Scout meetings twice a month. That was nothing compared to

Angelina's four-day-a week practice schedule *and* weekly games. Lydia made a mental note to call Sandra a wimp the next time she complained about her schedule. She and Angelina laughed when she told her about Sandra's constant complaining.

Once they were both satisfied with their purchases, Lydia and Angelina decided to do lunch at the Coney Island in the strip mall. After ordering, Angelina asked, "What else do you do outside of work, besides working out? Oh, yeah, and shopping?"

Lydia sipped her water before answering. "Not a whole lot, to tell you the truth. My two closest friends and I hang out once or twice a month for dinner, a movie, or a spa day. I spend time with my goddaughter. But nothing like hobbies or anything."

"So you really don't have a special man in your life, huh?" Angelina inquired.

"Until a few months ago, I was in a relationship. We spent quite a bit of time together, doing different things. Since that ended, I've really been focused on working towards a promotion in my job. That's been tying up evenings and weekends lately."

"Oh. What kind of position?" The short, fast moving waiter came back with their food. As they ate their grilled chicken salads, Lydia told Angelina all about the senior manager position after which Angelina asked, "So how's it looking for you?"

"The last I heard, I had it in the bag. I'm just hoping that a decision will be made soon. As a matter of fact, when I get home, I've got to finish up a report I'm working on for my boss."

They finished eating in silence. While walking to the parking lot, Angelina said, "It's too bad you're not seeing anyone special, because my husband and I like to hang out with other couples, and I really like you—in a non-lesbian kind of way," she added, winking. They both laughed.

"Yes, that would be nice. Truthfully, I've been seeing an ex of my mine for the last few weeks, but I'm not expecting that to last much longer."

Angelina's eyes narrowed at this tidbit of information. "Really! Why not?"

"Let's just say, I'm finally realizing why he's an ex." Angelina wanted to hear more, but they were interrupted by Lydia's cell phone ringing. The caller ID displayed a number she didn't recognize. When she answered, Officer Boyle announced himself immediately. Lydia signaled to Angelina that she had to take the call, and to give her a minute.

"Hi," she said. "I didn't think I'd hear from you so soon." Lydia put the last of her bags onto the back seat.

"I told you we'd get it done for you," he boasted. She could hear his smile through the phone. What a sexy smile it was, if she remembered correctly. Forcing herself to refocus on the business at hand, Lydia listened intently as Officer Boyle relayed the information they'd discovered. The person making the calls was definitely an amateur phone prankster, because all of the calls came from the same two numbers—a cell phone number and a residential number. He even had a name.

Lena Daniels. The name didn't ring a bell. Lydia had absolutely no idea who that was or why this person would begin harassing her out of nowhere.

"Any ideas?" Officer Boyle probed.

Lydia shook her head as though they were face to face and he could see her. Then she said aloud. "None."

"Think about it over the next couple of days. Maybe something'll come to you. I'll call you back in a couple days and see what you've come up with. Okay."

"No problem." Lydia responded before they said goodbye.

"Wow. What was that all about?" Angelina inquired.

Lydia filled her in briefly. Angelina shrugged. "Hmm. And you have no idea why this person would be doing this?"

"Of course not!" Lydia said frustrated.

Angelina sensed Lydia's frustration. "Okay. So what are your options?"

"I guess, if I want, I can have the police pick up this Lena Daniels for questioning and press charges. But I kind of want to figure this out on my own before I do all that."

"That sounds good. It's probably nothing to worry about anyway. Maybe this Lena Daniels has a bad sense of humor," Angelina suggested. This time they exchanged numbers before going their separate ways. Angelina insisted on checking up on Lydia. On the drive home, Lydia hoped that what Angelina said was true. But she had an unsettling feeling that there was much more to these calls than just someone having a little fun at her expense.

FOURTEEN

———✳———

By the first of October, fall had finally made its presence known. The leaves had already turned from the green of summer to the beautiful shades of browns and reds and had begun covering neatly mowed lawns. The temperature so far was holding steady in the forties and fifties.

Lydia was dressed in a cream colored, two-piece flared skirt, with a matching waist length jacket. She attended church service with her mother and Deacon George and was now on her way to have Sunday dinner at their house.

It would be awkward being in her mother's presence since the phone incident a couple of weeks ago. They'd had a few conversations since then, but nothing like their usual lighthearted, open mother-daughter talks. It was time for this to stop, Lydia decided. She figured that getting together after church would make things easier.

Wrong. She had never felt more uncomfortable in the house she'd grown up in, not since the time she thought that her mother could tell from looking at her that she had lost her virginity. Throughout dinner, Lydia fidgeted in the chair across from her mother's not-so-warm stare. She took small bites of the pot roast and baked potatoes that Caroline cooked as Deacon George tried to fill the awkward silence between mother and daughter with tidbits of church news.

Lydia had learned which church members were on the sick and shut-in list. She learned who had gone on to glory, and who all was on the prayer list. She wondered how much longer he'd be able to talk about church stuff before he ran out of things to say.

Caroline barely responded to her husband's conversation tactics, while Lydia offered nothing more than empty "um-hmms," and "oh reallys." Finally realizing that his efforts were futile, Deacon George gave up, excusing himself to go watch a football game in the den.

Quietly, Caroline stood from her chair, and began clearing the table. Instinctively, Lydia began to help. "You don't have to do that," Caroline stated stiffly.

Lydia sucked her teeth defiantly. Her mother was normally a mild-mannered, easy-going woman, but when she got *really* mad about something, she could hold on to a grudge for dear life. Lydia had been through enough of her mother's stints of anger during her teen years and beyond to know that she would have to be the one to initiate moving them past this.

"Okay, Ma." Lydia spoke softly. "I should have apologized before now, but I am sorry for what happened."

Caroline's voice was still hard, unmoved. "You're a grown woman. You don't owe me any apologies or explanations," she continued clearing the table pretending to not still be upset, Lydia knew better.

"I know I'm grown, Ma, but you raised me better than how I behaved."

"You're damn right you were raised better than that!" Her mother snapped suddenly, slamming the dishes she had in her hands on the table. "I don't know who you think you're fooling young lady. But it's certainly not me."

"Ma, what are you…." Lydia tried to interject, but Caroline cut her short.

"Only Thomas Cunningham can make you act like a *damn* fool," her mother declared bitterly. "I just don't understand what you're thinking, getting back involved with that man."

The hurt in her mother's voice ripped at the deepest part of Lydia's heart. It was the truth of her mother's words that hurt the worst. She should have known that she wouldn't be able to hide the truth from the woman who knew her better than anyone else.

Lydia moved in closer to her mother, throwing her arms around her. "Oh, Ma, I promise it's not what you think," Lydia cried.

Caroline pulled out of the embrace. "It's exactly what I think. My only guess is that you like being made a fool of, which is the only thing Thomas is good for—making a fool of you. Then again, maybe, it's you who's been making a fool of yourself all this time," she concluded, shaking her head shamefully.

Whoa! Lydia thought shockingly. Could there have been a truer statement? A thought she'd never even considered until the words spilled from her mother's lips just now. All the times she had been wronged by Thomas she always blamed him, ignoring her own involvement in the fate of their relationship.

"Maybe you're right, Ma. But I know what I'm doing this time."

"Yeah, what you're doing is messing up what you had with Roy, a good man, to play these games with Thomas." Caroline had never been this vocal about her feelings about Lydia and Thomas. "Why would you let that man back into your life, only to make a fool of you again? You're too smart for this. You're supposed to learn from the past, not keep repeating it."

"I'm not going to let that happen this time. I'm being careful this time," Lydia urged, wanting her mother to believe her.

"That's what you thought the last time," Caroline continued. She sat down at the kitchen table. "Don't you realize there shouldn't even be a 'this time' with him? When does it *stop* Lydia?" Caroline asked, exasperated.

"But Ma…" Lydia began.

"No! You listen to me, and you listen to me good, Lydia," Caroline said pointedly. "I won't have any part of what's going on with you and Thomas. I don't want to know anything about it! Whether you end up with a broken heart or not, I don't want to hear or know anything about it."

Upon her mother's departure from the kitchen, Lydia stood alone in the middle of the floor allowing the finality of her mother's words to settle in. When it was clear that Caroline had finished talking to her, Lydia kissed a quizzical looking Deacon George goodbye before she went home with a much heavier mind than when she arrived.

"Please, Auntie Liddy. I really want to go." Alicia was pleading into the phone. "I really want to go to the Halloween party. Why can't we go?" Alicia was whining so loudly that Lydia had to hold the phone a few inches away from her ear. As Alicia pleaded and pleaded, Lydia tried to come up with a clever excuse that Alicia would believe. There proved to be no such thing, so Lydia gave up trying.

Thomas had been complaining so much about her lack of availability to him that Lydia had finally agreed to give up this

Halloween weekend so that they could spend some time together outside of the bedroom. Although the bedroom had been the only place where things went right between them, Thomas claimed he wanted to show her that he could offer more than that. Otherwise, Lydia would have never considered canceling the annual event that she'd been taking Alicia to since she was two years old. Not only would she be disappointing Alicia, but she would also be disappointing Caroline, who looked forward to seeing Alicia at the party.

Rather than make up a reason for not going to the party, Lydia made a snap decision to go through with her usual plan to take Alicia to the party. The happiness and excitement that she heard in Alicia's voice reinforced that she had made the best decision. She could still hear Alicia's blissful shouting when Sandra returned to the phone.

"You know you were wrong pitting Alicia against me like that," Lydia jokingly complained to Sandra when she came back to the phone.

"Hey, you left me no choice. You know Alicia. She wasn't going to rest until one of us took her to that party. Sorry, love. It simply wasn't going to be me," Sandra explained coyly. "We both know you have no backbone when it comes to your goddaughter." They both laughed, knowing that was exactly why Lydia had left a voice message canceling their plans instead of talking to Alicia directly.

Lydia dialed Thomas' cell phone after settling with Sandra what time she'd be over to pick Alicia up. Six rings later, the voicemail finally came on, not surprising at all. More often than not, Lydia couldn't reach Thomas on his cell phone. It seemed that if he didn't call her, she was leaving him messages.

Ignoring her frustration at not being able to reach him directly, she left her message.

"Hi, Thomas, it's Lydia. I hope you get this message before you come over. I decided to go ahead and take Alicia to the party at the church. I just couldn't break her little heart. I hope you'll understand. I'll call you afterward."

Placing the phone on its base, Lydia was somewhat aggravated. She couldn't even count how many times she'd called his cell phone and had to leave messages. But Thomas always had an excuse—no signal, no power, it didn't ring—always something. It was no wonder she was beginning to feel suspicious. She was very well aware of the games that people played with their cell phones. Considering Thomas didn't have a good record for being on the up-and-up with her, Lydia didn't feel an ounce of guilt about her suspicions.

The time displayed on the DVD player was six o'clock. Lydia pulled herself up from her stretched out position on the couch to get ready so that she and Alicia could be at the party by seven. After her shower, she retrieved her old green M & M costume from the attic, glad that it wasn't too worn-out. Still, she made a plan to update her costume when they went on clearance after Halloween was over.

Almost out the door, Lydia heard her phone ringing from the kitchen. Just in case it was Alicia seeing if she had left the house, Lydia turned back to answer the phone.

"What the hell is this bullshit?" Thomas' angry voice boomed through the phone.

Lydia rolled her eyes at the phone. *"Excuse me!"* she replied. "Who are you talking to like that?"

He ignored her, continuing his demands. "You puttin' me off to play mommy to your friend's daughter?"

"First of all, I'm not *playing* mommy to anyone. I don't know what you think gives you the right to demand that I change my plans for you. You ought to be thanking me for calling you to let you know instead of pulling one of your numbers," Lydia snarled, not believing his utter nerve.

"You know, Lydia. I'm getting a little tired of you throwing my past mistakes in my face. Now, you started fucking with me again for *some* reason. So *something* about me must be *right.*" Thomas sounded more bigheaded than she had ever heard him, and he wasn't finished. "If you're just using your friend's daughter as an excuse to go see somebody else, why don't you be woman enough to just put it out there."

It was official. Thomas surely had lost his mind. It was clear that Lydia needed to put him in his place. "Thomas," she began pointedly, "let me be clear. I may be *fucking* you for old time's sake, but don't get it twisted—you are *not* my man. The last thing I need to do is make excuses if I want to see someone else. I don't owe you any explanations or anything else, for that matter. And since you have such a fucked up attitude, don't hold your breath waiting for a phone call from me tonight."

FIFTEEN

———◈———

On the drive to Sandra's house, Lydia was still fuming over Thomas's audacity. He obviously hadn't realized that she was nowhere near the same timid, always agreeable young woman he was used to dealing with in their past. He'd broken her heart too many times for her to give him the privileges he once had. In the past, she wouldn't have given a second thought to canceling her plans with Alicia, or anybody else for that matter, simply because he wanted her to. Now, he wasn't worth it.

Her thoughts drifted to her mother's words about her part of the blame for how things were with Thomas. Caroline was right. A man can only do to you what you allow him to do, Lydia hated to admit. The reason Thomas thought she should've dropped everything for him was because that was the precedent she had set.

But, like she had told her mother, she was determined to do things differently this time, and so far, she had. She wasn't letting Thomas come in and disrupt her life completely like he had done before, even though, his sheer presence had her lying and sneaking around, and keeping him a secret from those closest to her. Again, those were her choices.

No one made her refuse Roy's marriage proposal. No one made her give in to the monstrous sexual attraction she had for Thomas. And no one made her lie to her family and friends. Those were all decisions she had made on her own. No one was holding a gun to her head.

Lydia caught sight of the troubled expression in her eyes in the rearview mirror as she checked traffic in the lane next to her, preparing to exit the freeway. It was time for her to make some tough decisions—decisions that should have been made a long time ago.

Lydia reasoned that she started seeing Thomas again more out of habit than anything else. The only good thing that came from it was confirmation of how much she'd grown, and that she realized that she deserved, and wanted, more. She wanted something better than she could ever have with Thomas.

Finally, she was realizing that what she and Thomas had together was good for what it was, and most importantly, when it was. Thomas was responsible for igniting the woman inside of her. He was the first man to expose her heart to feelings of love and affection, and inconceivable passion. For that, he would always be special, someone who no one could ever replace—her first love. But that was the past. And that's where it needed to stay.

Arriving at Sandra's house, Lydia pushed thoughts of Thomas out of her mind, and decided to find a way out of the mess she had created later. Once inside, Alicia all but tackled an unsuspecting Lydia, knocking the wind out of her.

"Whoa, baby girl! You'd better watch that before you mess up my costume," Lydia teased, but Alicia wasn't buying it.

"It's not like it's real or something." Alicia was adorably decked out in a clown costume, white painted face, and large black nose, with widely drawn-on red lips, compliments of her artistic mother.

"You are just too cute for words," Lydia cooed over her, sending a monstrously wide smile across Alicia's lips.

"Thank you," Alicia replied, smiling. "You're cute too."

"Yeah, yeah, yeah," Sandra broke in. "No compliments for the butterball mommy over here," Sandra said, joining them in the living room. Sandra's belly did seem to have expanded considerably since Lydia saw her last, but Lydia knew better than to say as much.

"Whatever, girl! You know you still got it going on, BIG MOMMA," Lydia teased, patting Sandra's belly, which she knew pregnant women hated and loved simultaneously. Sandra smirked, then hugged Alicia before she and Lydia left.

The fellowship hall of the church was expertly decorated for the occasion—artificial cobwebs, plastic spiders and bats hanging from the ceiling. There were tables set up along the four walls of the room—one for food, one for drawing, and one for each of the games the kids would be playing. In one of the corners was a television set and DVD player with some age-appropriate scary movies for the older kids who had brought their younger siblings to the party.

In an effort to keep kids safe indoors instead of being in the streets on Halloween, the church had been hosting the party for the past six years. Each year the party had grown in popularity, not only for the children in the church, but also for the children in the surrounding neighborhood. Caroline was president of the youth committee and was extremely proud of its success.

Lydia and Alicia had been at the party for about thirty minutes before she finally found her mother, Caroline, frantically running around, keeping everything operating smoothly.

Caroline didn't do the costume thing, so she was extra casually dressed in loose fitting blue jeans, printed tee, covered with an orange smock tied loosely at the sides.

"Hi, baby, don't you look cute?" Caroline greeted Lydia with a much-needed hug. Although mother and daughter were back on speaking terms, there was still tension between them. So Lydia welcomed the sincerity of her mother's embrace. "And where's my grandbaby?" Caroline asked, looking around.

"Oh, Ma, you know there was no keeping up with that girl once we got in here. She disappeared with a bunch of her friends." Lydia said, looking around herself for Alicia. Even knowing that Alicia was in good company, she kept a watchful eye on her. Having spotted her, Lydia pointed Alicia out to her mother, who immediately smiled, which brightened Lydia's heart.

"I won't bother her now. I'm sure she'll give me a hug once she sees me." Someone was calling Caroline's name from across the room. Before she left, she turned back to Lydia. "Hey, you can make yourself useful for the night. I need you to work the apple-bobbing game table for me. We're short a few volunteers."

"No problem," she answered speedily, but Caroline had already begun walking away to help the chip person before the boxes went crashing to the floor. Lydia began walking in the direction of the game tables. Along the way, she was greeted with tight hugs and wet kisses from many of the church members she hadn't seen in a while. With all of the 'we miss you's' and 'long time no sees', Lydia was soon promising to be at church, front and center, the next Sunday.

As Lydia neared the apple-bobbing table, she was rushed by three little boys, dressed like Power Ranger characters, who she immediately recognized. "Heyyyy, Ms. Lydia," they sang, far from in unison. She instinctively hugged them back. They were like her little nephews.

"My boys!" It had been at least a year since she'd seen them. Kevin, Tyrone, and Devon were the children of Roy's younger sister, Deborah, who lived in Texas. Deborah finally decided to give up on having a daughter after having her third son. So whenever Deborah visited, Lydia knew she had to give up some time with Alicia because, Deborah looked forward to playing mommy to her for as long as she could, and spoiling Alicia as much as everybody else did. It was odd, though, that Sandra hadn't mentioned that Deborah was in town.

"Where's your mom?" Lydia questioned, scanning the room.

The boys didn't have a chance to respond. A familiar voice suddenly came from behind her. "They're here with their favorite uncle."

Without looking behind her, Lydia knew that the voice belonged to Roy. "Ohmigod!" she screamed when she finally turned to face him. Roy's normally handsome face was disguised with a gruesome mask with fake, but very real-looking blood dripping all over. She punched him playfully in the chest, being reminded, instantly, of the muscular body he maintained. Shamefully, she remembered where she was, and forced those thoughts from her mind. "I can't believe you, Roy!" He knew she couldn't stand being scared.

Pulling the mask up to the top of his head, Roy's boyish smile was revealed. "What can I say? I couldn't help myself," he explained. "You know I'm just a kid at heart. I probably had my costume before the kids," he added, showcasing his already filled bag of goodies.

"Yes, you've made that pretty obvious," she said, smirking.

"Looks like you're in the same boat," Roy said, eyeing her costume.

"Well, Alicia wouldn't let me come otherwise." Their eyes met, just for a moment. Roy broke the gaze, causing an unsettling feeling in Lydia's stomach. Reverting back to the kids, she asked, "When did Deborah and the kids get here?"

Seemingly glad to be back on a neutral path, he said, "Deborah's not here. I'd been visiting them for the past few weeks. Since she and Mike are always complaining about not having enough quality time together, I offered to bring the boys back with me for a couple of weeks."

His explanation wasn't surprising to Lydia at all. Roy was always doing stuff like that for his loved ones. He'd always been a dependable, helpful person to those he cared for. Another wonderful characteristic she had walked away from.

"Only, I didn't quite know what I was getting myself into," he continued. "These boys are definitely a handful, to say the least. But they don't drive me crazy enough to steer me away from wanting a couple of my own." Their eyes met again. Only this time, Roy didn't turn away. He held her eyes until she couldn't take it anymore, not being able to handle the implication of his stare.

"Uhmm…I better get going. I'm on assignment for my mom," she said, starting to walk away. She noticed Roy walking in the same direction. "You following me now?"

"No." he said quizzically. "At least I'm not trying to. I'm on my way to the apple bobbing table," Roy claimed.

"You're kidding right?" Lydia exclaimed incredulously. This was none other than the work of her mother, conveniently putting the two of them together at the same table. After informing Roy of where she was going, they laughed at her mother's craftiness, then headed to the table.

By the end of the night Lydia and Roy were having as much fun as the kids. Their participation didn't stop with the apple bobbing table. They helped judge the screaming contest, after which they pretended to get into a tussle over who the winner was. The kids really got a laugh out of that.

They ended up helping to make plates for the kids, then handing out goody bags at the end of the party. Whatever awkwardness was there between them at the beginning of the night had dissipated. They were having so much fun with the kids, it felt like old times, when things were less complicated. It was that kind of fun and excitement between them that began their friendship so many years before.

Lydia was having so much fun with Roy, reveling in how well he interacted with the kids—really letting the kid within himself come alive. The more time she spent with him, the farther Thomas drifted from her mind, making her even more satisfied that she'd blown him off for the night. She was sure she wouldn't have had nearly as much fun.

"Tonight was really fun," Lydia smiled, making sure a well-exhausted Alicia was securely fastened in her seatbelt once they made it out to the car. The boys were already asleep and buckled up inside Roy's car. She and Roy were standing outside her truck. Both of them had taken their costumes off before leaving out of the church. He was parked beside her.

"It was for me, too," Roy replied bashfully. "I'm glad I came." His hands were fidgeting at his sides. He wanted to say more, but he was holding back. "Lydia, I need to apologize for ignoring you after our run-in at your mother's."

"Don't worry about it. You had every reason not to want to talk to me," she admitted. "I just wanted to clear things up about Thomas. You see…"

Roy cut her short. "I don't care about Thomas, Lydia. You're who I care about." His expression, at the mention of Thomas' name, hardened. When he spoke of her, his expression softened. "It's getting late. We both need to get these kids in the bed. I hope you don't mind, but I dropped a letter by your house before I came here. It will do a better job of expressing what I want to say than what I'd be able to do tonight. Just read it, think about it, and call me in a few days, okay?"

"Sure." She was stunned. No other words came to mind. Taking her by surprise, Roy kissed her gently before ushering her into her truck. Like a true gentleman, he waited for her to leave before he got inside his car and pulled away behind her.

After seeing Alicia safely home, Lydia's ride home was a blur. Her heart began racing the closer she got to home, anticipating Roy's letter. More than likely his words would be heartfelt, sincere, and forthcoming. Roy wasn't the type to hold back when he really wanted something. The fact that he'd even written her a letter after their last encounter was a sign that he wasn't letting her go without giving it his all. He'd always believed they were meant to be, she remembered him telling her on more than one occasion. Lydia had begun feeling the same way, until Thomas came back, bringing confusion with him.

Finally, she was home. Hurriedly, she pulled into the driveway, shifted the truck in park, then jumped out. Anxiety filled her every step, until she reached her front door.

"Where the fuck have you been?" Fire was burning in Thomas' eyes as he pushed her forcibly against the door. His face was hard and angry.

Stunned, Lydia was unable to find her voice. *What the hell was this all about?* Pain surged through her arms in response to the tight grip he had on her. "What the hell are you talking about?" Lydia winced in pain.

"ANSWER MY FUCKIN' QUESTION!" His voice was thunderous and his tone threatening as he applied even more pressure, until finally she crumpled to the ground. Frightened, she said a quick prayer. She didn't know what else to do. She'd never been handled in such a rough manner.

"Thomas, you're hurting me," Lydia pleaded, trying desperately to reason with this stranger before her. "You already know where I was tonight."

He released her arms, leaving her to pull herself up off the ground. This would be the ideal time for a nosy neighbor to stick their nose where it didn't belong and call the police.

"I've been letting you dog me for the last few months, but I'm not stupid, so drop the innocent act," he thundered. "I know that damn church party was over by nine o'clock—it's almost eleven thirty. So where the hell have you been for the last two hours?" Thomas demanded.

Lydia couldn't help thinking how ironic it was that *he* didn't like the feeling of being toyed with, when that's all he did with her. But she knew better than to mention that tidbit of information now. Instead she tried to calm him down by explaining herself. "I helped clean up the church, Thomas. Then I dropped Alicia off at home."

Thomas never took his angry eyes off of her. "Cleaning up, huh?" Thomas mocked, furiously. "What does cleaning up have to do with you out in the parking lot kissing on your little letter-writing, *pussy* of an ex-boyfriend." He flung a crumpled piece of paper at her face, which she could only assume was the letter Roy told her about.

Ohmigod! Lydia couldn't believe that Thomas had been at the church watching her. Her skin crawled at the thought. As the paper found its place at her feet, Lydia became furious. How dare he come back into her life making demands of her, trying to take up all of her free time, and now invading her right to privacy? He had absolutely no right to question her about anything—who she was sleeping with, how late she stayed out, or why her ex was doing anything.

Where the courage came from to stand up to Thomas' insane behavior, she didn't know, but she was glad for it.

"I don't know who you think you are. But it's none of your *damn* business why I just got home or what I was doing with *whomever!*" Lydia turned to put her key in the entry door. She stepped inside, leaving a stunned Thomas on the porch. "It's crystal clear that this—whatever it is—is not working between us."

"Don't say that, Lydia." Thomas said, quickly regaining his composure, but it was too late. "You're just not giving us the chance we deserve 'cause you're trying to be so hard and shit. I *know* that's not you, baby. You know that's not you," he pleaded. "If you go back to the Lydia you used to be, everything would be just right."

Without hesitation, she shot back, "The *old* Lydia was the problem..."

"I won't let you go, Lydia." Before she could close the door on him, he pushed through, grabbing hold of her. She tried pulling away, but he wouldn't let her. Hungrily, he covered her lips with his. His kisses lured her into him until she found herself wrapped up in the passion, returning his kisses until they melted into mutual pleasure in the middle of her living room floor.

SIXTEEN

T he word floating around is that you're the "it" girl for the senior manager position, baby girl." Lydia and Marianne were behind the closed doors of Marianne's corner office on the fifteenth floor, where all the executive offices were located. Her office was impeccably decorated with a cream-colored Italian leather sectional, freshly shined oak desk, and with lamb skin desk chairs on top of the softest, most plush carpet that Lydia had ever walked on in her life. The walls were adorned with paintings by some of the world's most famous African American artists. Lydia was in awe whenever she walked inside, which wasn't very often.

Usually Marianne came down to the twelfth floor to Lydia's office if she wanted to talk, or they instant messaged each other. But this was good news that she wanted to share face-to-face, with a little more privacy than they would've gotten in Lydia's office. Whenever Marianne made a visit to the lower level offices, it always created a buzz. All eyes and ears were on her and whoever she was visiting. Discretion was of high priority with something like this. Officially, the decision had not been announced, but Marianne was often privy to important facts before the details were released. After holding her tongue a week after hearing the news herself, she couldn't keep it from Lydia any longer. Plus, she had spilled the beans to Denise and knew it was only a matter of time before Denise flapped her jaws. And letting Lydia hear the news from anyone but her was not an option.

Springing excitedly from her chair, Lydia rushed over to Marianne and threw her arms around her, careful not to wrinkle the pinstriped Christian Dior pant suit jacket. "Are you serious?" Lydia asked, rhetorically, knowing Marianne wouldn't play around about this. "I can't believe it!"

"Sure you can. You're just being modest. You've really been about your business, handling everything that's been thrown your way. Just stay on that path and I guarantee it's yours. The official announcement will be made in a couple of weeks."

"So what you're really saying is, I can't get the BIG HEAD yet, huh?" Lydia joked, returning to her seat on the other side of Marianne's desk. They talked for a few more minutes, made plans for a pre-celebratory lunch that afternoon, and then Lydia sashayed back down to her own office.

Back in her office, Lydia was still ecstatic over the news she'd received from Marianne. Even though it was hush-hush news, she knew Sandra wasn't included in that, so she made immediate plans to drop by her house after work to share it with her.

Her mood spiraled downward as her thoughts turned to Thomas. Since the weekend of the Halloween party two weeks ago, after she told him things weren't working between them, it was like he heard just the opposite. Seriously! He revved it up into overdrive. He sent flowers to her job, and her house, and text messages of "I love you," "I'm sorry," and "Don't give up."

His calls were endless. "Just to let you know, I'm thinking of you," he'd say. Not answering his calls only made matters worse. He'd keep calling. In one day, she had over fifty missed calls, all from Thomas.

Thomas was acting so desperate; it was becoming scary. She'd never seen him act like this before. He was usually so laid back, and blasé about everything. In the past, it had always been she who'd been so hard pressed over their relationship. Funny how the tables had turned.

Too bad they hadn't changed sooner. If they had, maybe Lydia wouldn't have felt compelled to put things on the back burner with Roy.

Lydia rang Sandra's doorbell for the third time. Still, no answer. Strange. Sandra's car was in the driveway. Of course, considering that she was pregnant, Lydia could easily assume that Sandra had fallen asleep. Only that wasn't likely, since she had told Sandra what time she'd be coming by after work. Trying not to read too much into the situation, Lydia turned to leave just as Alicia cracked the door with sadness in her eyes.

"Hey, sweetie," Lydia said quietly. "What took so long for you to open the door?"

"Mommy said not to open the door. She said she doesn't feel like company. Not even you."

Assuming something was going on between Sandra and Lester, Lydia told Alicia not to worry, that her mom was probably just not having a good day. "Go on back inside and tell your mom I'll call her later." She made sure Alicia closed and locked the door before she got back into her truck.

Buzzzzzz. It was her cell phone vibrating inside her purse. Seated in her truck, shifting the gear into reverse to pull out of Sandra's driveway, Lydia reached into her purse while checking for any oncoming cars on the quiet residential block.

"Hello." It was Kania. Probably calling to give her a list of things she needed her to do in preparation of the upcoming bridal shower. But, Kania's tone wasn't filled with her usual chirpiness, but instead with the seriousness she used more with clients. She must have heard news about Lena Daniels, she reasoned. Through connections her law firm had with the police department, Lydia had passed the information from Officer Boyle to Kania to see what she could find out. That was a couple of weeks ago. The hang up calls coincidentally stopped right after Lydia had gotten the name from Officer Boyle, but she still had to find out what the motive was, if any, behind the calls in the first place. If the minor harassment had ended with phone calls and a brick hadn't been thrown through her window, Lydia could have left it alone. Somehow the window incident suggested something personal. That's what Lydia hoped to find out about.

"Hi, Lydia." Kania's tone was flat. "I've got some information. But this is something we need to discuss in person. I'm in your neighborhood. Are you home or close to it?" Something was wrong. Kania's tone was entirely too icy, like she was angry or something. Lydia was less than five minutes away from her house.

Lydia saw Kania's car as soon as she turned the corner to her street. Kania was parked on the street in front of her house. Through the window, Kania's expression was angry. *What the hell is this all about?* Lydia wondered nervously as she pulled in the driveway, walking to the front door. Kania followed, awkwardly silent.

Not apologizing for the messy condition of her living room, Lydia spoke abruptly. "What the hell is going on here, Kania? First, Sandra tells Alicia not to open the door for me. Now you're acting all cold towards me. What does this have to do with what you have for me?"

Kania was professionally dressed in a navy blue pant suit, hair swooped up into a perfect French twist. Disappointment and anger seeped through her eyes. She spoke in her lawyerly fashion, pointedly. "You want to know what everybody's problem is, Lydia?

It's you." Kania stood up and, walked towards Lydia, holding a manila folder in her hand She flung it at her. "You are the problem."

"What*?*" Lydia was confused, sliding the papers, which had scattered across the floor, back into the folder.

Kania interjected, angrily. "You've been lying to your best friends. Having us all worried about you and these phone calls, then the brick thrown through your window. And why? Because you can't stop *fucking* around with Thomas!"

Stunned, Lydia couldn't believe what she'd just heard. This wasn't at all how she wanted her friends to find out. She knew exactly what they would think. Absolutely nothing had gone according to her *stupid* plan.

"Look at you," Kania spat, waving her finger accusatorily at Lydia. "You don't even have anything to say. You brought all of this shit on yourself. And for a man that you know ain't shit! What the hell is wrong with you?"

Lydia managed to compose herself enough to finally speak. "Yes. I started seeing Thomas again. I knew you and Sandra would have a fit if you knew. But I swear I was going to tell you after…"

"After what, Lydia? After he dumps you again, letting you think he's going to marry you. Again." Kania was beyond angry. Lydia hadn't ever seen her fuming like this.

"No," Lydia screeched, wishing she could say something to make her appear less like an idiot. There was nothing. "I…uh…," she stammered. She threw her hands up towards her white stucco ceilings. "What does this have to do with Lena Daniels?"

"Everything." Kania retrieved the folder from the coffee table. She tossed it at Lydia, who caught it on cue. "Lena Daniels is Thomas' wife. The bastard is married, Lydia. You've been fucking around with a married man. His wife found out and started fucking with you. That's the gist of it. It's all in the file. Look at it for yourself."

The room was spinning. *Married!* The word swirled around in her head. *Thomas. Married. How? When?*

Kania broke through the shock of the news. "Oh. Don't think he just got married either. He's been married for like seven years. They have a son, too."

"Ohmigod!" Lydia muffled, plopping down on the couch. She turned away from Kania. "I swear, I didn't know about any of this."

"It doesn't even matter whether you knew or not. You had no business getting involved with him again. And it says a lot about what your friends mean to you for you to get into this and not even tell us about it. It's not supposed to matter whether we'll like what you're doing or not. Friends don't keep secrets. Or maybe I should say, *real* friends." Kania gathered her things and left Lydia standing alone in the middle of her floor, tears streaming down her face.

SEVENTEEN

hree days later, Lydia was still processing the news she'd received from Kania. She couldn't even make it out of bed, let alone to work. Every bone in her body ached from all the heaving, huffing, puffing, and crying that she'd been doing since Kania left her standing in the middle of her living room floor.

Lying in bed underneath the multicolored comforter set, her head was pounding. Had been for the past twenty minutes since she'd first opened her eyes. Carefully pulling the covers from over her head, she scanned the room for the Motrin caplets that she had been popping everyday for a rash of aches and pains that she'd been experiencing. Regretfully, they weren't immediately in sight.

"Dammit!" Lydia cursed, having raised her head too quickly, finally managing to get her legs out of the bed and onto the floor. Slowly, with each carefully orchestrated step she took towards the bathroom, her head pounded worse. The medicine she needed was nowhere in sight when she opened the medicine cabinet. Angrily, she slammed the door shut, not caring about the toothpaste and dental floss that had fallen out before the door closed.

Maybe this horrific headache she had was just what she deserved for being such a fool. A fool for Thomas. A fool for being a terrible friend to Sandra and Kania, as well as a terrible daughter to her mother, all those who cared the most about her. Sadly, she remembered that Roy was on that list too as she climbed back into bed, massaging her temples for some kind of relief.

She continued scanning the room in search of the Motrin bottle she knew was somewhere in the mess of her bedroom. *Just one tablet*, she thought. One tablet would do the trick. It always did. But when her eyes came upon that manila folder containing all the years of lies and deceit that Thomas had brought her way, the pounding instantly worsened.

It sickened her to think that the reality of her involvement with Thomas could have been much worse than some prank phone calls and a brick through her window, as if that wasn't bad enough. This wife of his—Lena Daniels—obviously wasn't afraid of going to great lengths to protect what was hers. Who knew what could have been next in her bag of tricks?

Lydia had spent the last few days reading and rereading through the devastation contained in the file. No matter how many times she read the material, it still read the same—unbelievable.

Thomas had married Lena the same year he and Lydia started dating, only a few months later. Their son, Thomas Jr., was also born that same year. Marriage and birth certificates confirmed everything. What kind of man does something like this? Not only to her, but to his wife, and to his child. It'd be different if he and Lydia had just had a one-night stand or something. But Thomas had been living a double life. A single man to Lydia. Husband and father to Lena and their son.

With thoughts of Thomas and his betrayal swirling around in her head, Lydia drifted back off to sleep, awaking shortly after noon. Thank God the headache had passed. But there seemed to be no end in sight to the hurt in her heart.

What hurt her more than Thomas having deceived her all of these years, was the disappointment she brought to those closest to her—her mother and her friends. They expected better judgment from her, especially after all this time. More than that, they expected trust and honesty. And she deceived them all, trying to shield herself against their criticisms. In the end, she only hurt them.

A message from Marianne is what finally got Lydia out of bed. "Alright, honey. Don't let the pending promotion go so much to your head that you stop coming to work. Since I know nothing is going on with your family, it can only be a man that's brought this on. Like Mariah said baby, "Shake it ooofff," she sang. "A man can only break your heart, not your spirit. So I expect to see you back in here tomorrow morning," she concluded matter-of-factly.

Marianne's matter-of-factness was jolting, hard-hitting. She was right, reminding Lydia that her heart wasn't so much broken over learning of Thomas' deceit, because her heart hadn't gotten deeply involved. Over the past few weeks, she had already come to the decision that there was nothing significant between her and Thomas anyway. It was more anger that she was feeling. Anger because he was going to do the same thing to her that he had done before.

By two o'clock, Lydia had showered and dressed for the chilly November day in a black and turquoise sweat suit. She swooped her hair up in a ponytail, then proceeded to bring some neatness and order to her house. Two hours later she felt as though she could breathe again. Lydia cleaned the house from top to bottom, starting with her bedroom, then the kitchen, and then laundry.

Finally, Lydia realized that she couldn't put it off any longer. She needed to make amends with her friends for leaving them in the dark, not trusting them with the truth. She left both of them messages to meet her for drinks at one of their favorite restaurants at five.

Arriving at Fishbone's near the five o'clock hour, Lydia was seated immediately at a corner table in the non-smoking section. For starters, she ordered three ice waters with fresh lemons. Kania joined her a few minutes later. Her mood was casual, yet aloof. The ladies greeted each other kindly. An awkward silence lingered after the waiter delivered their waters, and they waited for Sandra to show up. Fifteen minutes later, Kania spoke up.

"Sandra called me and said she wasn't coming. I thought I convinced her otherwise, but it doesn't look like it," she admitted, reluctantly.

Lydia inhaled deeply, disappointment settling upon her. "Well, I guess I'm not really in a position to get mad."

Kania shrugged her shoulders. "You know Sandra. It's going to take some time for her. What you did, on top of everything else she's dealing with, really hurt her feelings.

That made Lydia feel even worse. She hadn't given much thought to how her friends were going to feel when they did find out. And finding out the way they did only made it worse. "I guess I really just wanted you guys to know that I didn't know he was married. I would never have been seeing him if I knew that."

"You do know that's not the point, though, Lydia," Kania interjected in her lawyerly tone. "You shouldn't have been seeing him at all."

"Yes, but I still wanted you to know that I was not knowingly seeing a married man," Lydia explained. While she felt good opening up to Kania, her heart was crushed that Sandra didn't even want to face her. "I'm really sorry I didn't tell you guys from the beginning about Thomas. I knew you wouldn't want to be bothered with me and this foolishness with him, even though I had something completely different in mind."

She explained further to Kania about the conclusions she had come to on her own about her relationship with Thomas, and how she knew he had never been any good for her. Kania was relieved to hear that. Over appetizers and Margarita's, Kania accepted Lydia's apology and made her promise to never keep her or Sandra in the dark about anything serious going on in her life, promising that the next time she would not be so forgiving. Lydia wasted no time agreeing to the terms of their renewed friendship.

"And don't worry about Sandra," Kania reassured her as they prepared to leave. "She may make it hard for you, but she loves you *more* than a sister and she'll get over it."

That much Lydia knew was true. On the way home, she stopped by Sandra's house. Again, no answer. At least this time, though, there were no cars in the driveway. That didn't mean Sandra's car couldn't have been in the garage and she was just avoiding Lydia again, but at least it wasn't blatant avoidance, if that were the case.

Besides, Sandra couldn't avoid her forever. Thanksgiving was less than two weeks away, the bridal shower the week after that. They were bound to see each other at one, or both, of the events.

The rest of the day Lydia spent relaxing at home. She couldn't let herself stay down over this situation. She was stronger than that. In due time, everything would be back to normal. Then Thomas would be a true thing of the past.

Lydia was faced now with what to do with the information she had learned about Thomas. Either she could confront him, or leave him holding the bag with no explanation, not knowing what the hell happened. He'd given her plenty of experiences with that. It would serve him right. Having made her decision, she felt no remorse skipping through the messages he left on her voicemail and deleting them. "Who cares what you have to say?" she said aloud.

The Thanksgiving holiday came and went uneventfully. The only things missing from the festivities were Sandra and Alicia, who always dropped by, if even for a few minutes. Lydia didn't give up hope of them coming until her mother started clearing the leftover food from the table. Just as Lydia was thinking that Sandra must have really been upset to risk disappointing her mother, Caroline explained that Sandra had called earlier to express her regrets for not being able to make it. She had been experiencing some pretty heavy Braxton Hicks contractions and headaches.

"I thought she would have already told you," Caroline said, clearly surprised.

Caroline understood completely when Lydia confessed what she had learned about Thomas and how she had kept her involvement with him a secret from Sandra and Kania.

"Didn't I tell you that man was nothing but trouble?" Her mother scolded her. Even though she had said she didn't want to hear anything about Thomas, Caroline would always be a shoulder for her daughter to lean on, although Lydia assured her that she was fine. That Lydia already knew, before everything came out that Thomas wasn't the one for her. Her mother's face showed how glad she was to hear those words come from Lydia's mouth.

"What about Roy?" Lydia should have expected that question, but she didn't. Not only that, but she also didn't have an answer for it. It would be no surprise if her mother was aware of the letter Roy had written to her, or the fact that Lydia hadn't spoken to him about it. "A man is only going to be so patient with you, Lydia. No matter how much he loves you," her mother said before Lydia left for home.

Lydia drove home reflecting on those very words, knowing without any doubt that she had made a huge mistake breaking up with

Roy. She was afraid that if the truth about Thomas was revealed to Roy before she had a chance to explain things to him in her own way, her chances of fixing things between them were slim to none.

EIGHTEEN

---※---

The weekend of the bridal shower had finally arrived, and Lydia couldn't have been happier for Kania. Everything was going perfectly according to plan, with the exception that she and Sandra were still somewhat estranged. Only through contact with Kania did she learn that Sandra still believed that Lydia knew all along that Thomas was married and continued seeing him anyway. That was the only logical explanation for her need for such secrecy, even from her best friends.

At a chance run-in at Kania's, midweek before the bridal shower, Lydia tried to get Sandra to talk to her, but she wouldn't budge. She didn't want to alarm Alicia that anything was wrong between herself and Sandra, so Lydia tried to act normally, directing her attention to Alicia when Sandra averted her eyes away from her.

"Auntie, when am I going to spend the weekend with you again?" Alicia asked innocently when Lydia walked with her and Sandra to their car.

"Real soon, sweetie," Lydia responded assuredly, before Sandra drove away not acknowledging her presence.

Kania watched the scene play out from her front door. Lydia was there to pick up the last minute to-do list for the shower. She wasn't quite sure what Sandra, whose due date was quickly approaching, was doing there. Sandra was basically just going to make an appearance at the shower, since she was at the point in her pregnancy where minimal activity was recommended.

Handing Lydia the professionally typed list through the door, Kania said kindly, speaking of Sandra, "Don't even worry about that pregnant woman. Once she drops that load, she'll be so happy, your foolishness will be a thing of the past."

That could be as many as three to four more weeks away. Lydia wasn't about to have it go even close to that long. She was going to squash this by the end of the shower, Lydia assured herself.

Completing the last of the items on the to-do list except picking up the cake, which she decided she would do on the way to Vanessa's clubhouse, Lydia made a quick stop at Nu-Creation Hair Salon to see her longtime friend and hair stylist, Darlene. A forty-something, petite, still shapely woman, Darlene was standing in front of her current client, creating a swoop like curl with the steaming curling iron when Lydia sashayed through the doors.

For this to be a Friday afternoon, Lydia noticed that the shop was not filled with its usual clientele of chatterbox professional women who rushed in after work trying to beat the Saturday morning crowd. Including the young woman Darlene was working on, there was only one other client there sitting under the dryer.

"Where's everybody?" Lydia inquired.

"Oh no, honey," Darlene began in her usual southern drawl. "I saved this weekend just for your friend's bridal party. I only scheduled my regulars for today."

One of Lydia's wedding gifts to Kania was taking care of the bridal party's hair and nails. It was costing her a pretty penny, but doing it for a great friend like Kania was more than gratifying. Besides, Lydia knew that if the shoe was on the other foot, Kania would do something of equal or greater value for her. But judging from how Lydia was handling things with Roy, the time wouldn't be coming any time soon.

Before saying goodbye to Darlene one hour and a fresh hair-do later, Lydia confirmed the time of the appointments for tomorrow, and then headed home to get some rest before getting ready for the shower. She needed to calm down. She felt slightly anxious about how she was going to approach Sandra regarding this "Thomas" issue, as well as make sure the shower was perfect.

Lydia awoke groggy from her nap, which had been all of twenty minutes. The clock on her mantel read two-thirty. Lydia splashed water over her face before taking a quick shower. The weather was unseasonably warm for Michigan being so close to Christmas, Lydia dressed in an ankle-length cream, sleeveless sweater dress with a matching tunic sweater. She accented the ensemble with chocolate colored, slingback pumps, and simple, gold teardrop earrings.

Traffic was so clear that Lydia felt as though she owned the freeway, zipping between lanes at her leisure. Her time on the freeway was usually stressful because it was always during rush hour traffic. This feeling was a luxury not often afforded to her.

In perfect timing, she picked up the cake from Lucille's Bakery and arrived at Vanessa's apartment complex at the same time as Sandra. She knew it was Sandra because only Alicia would be waving wildly in her direction from the backseat of a seemingly brand new martini-red Mercedes. *Hmm, must be a make-up gift from Lester*, Lydia thought shamefully. "If he really wants forgiveness, he should try being faithful to his wife."

"You see my mommy's new car, Auntie?" Alicia asked gleefully. She was properly dressed in a lighter style winter jacket.

Unsuccessfully trying to gauge Sandra's mood, Lydia complimented her. "I sure do. It is quite sharp." Sending Alicia a few feet away to ring Vanessa's buzzer to let her know that she and Sandra were there, Lydia retrieved the cake from her back seat. She watched Sandra, who still hadn't bothered acknowledging her presence, retrieve a box containing extra paper products, streamers, balloons, and other such decorative doodads. Vanessa came out of her complex just as Lydia and Sandra reached the door. Rather than taking them up to her apartment only to have to bring them back down, Vanessa took them directly over to the clubhouse, where the festivities were to take place in a few hours.

As soon as Alicia was out of earshot, Lydia cornered Sandra, who was about to excuse herself to Vanessa's apartment to get some more decorations.

"That can wait." Lydia began sternly. "But this," she said knowingly, "has gone on long enough."

All of the anger Sandra had been holding onto began slithering from her tongue. "No. What's gone on long enough is your foolishness, your sneaking around, and your lying. That's what's gone on long enough! So don't call yourself checking me. I have every right to be pissed with you!" Like pregnant women often do, Sandra rested her hands on top of her huge belly as she sauntered to the other side of the round table the two of them were standing next to.

Lydia knew she would need to tread softly with Sandra, not wanting to send her into labor from experiencing intense emotions. The last thing she wanted to be responsible for was Sandra going into labor at Kania's bridal shower, no matter how memorable it would have been later on. Her tone was calm when she responded.

"Sandra, I'm not saying that you don't have a right to be angry with me, because you do," Lydia said, meaning every word. Since Sandra was the one responsible for Lydia and Roy meeting in the first place, it was understandable that she'd take it more personally than anyone else that it looked like Lydia had dumped Roy for Thomas.

"I shouldn't have kept what was going on away from you." Lydia closed the gap between herself and Sandra. She placed her hand softly on Sandra's shoulder as she continued. "But you have to believe that I had no idea about this marriage stuff until Kania told me."

"Why should I believe that?" Sandra shot back in a raised voice. "You've been doing all this lying to me, Kania, and your mother, I'm sure. It only makes sense that you'd lie about not knowing that he was married."

"I don't care about what makes sense, Sandra. I know I haven't been honest, but I'm not lying about this. I would never knowingly involve myself with a married man. Not even Thomas."

Vanessa and Alicia entered the clubhouse and interrupted their exchange, announcing the arrival of the caterer. It was four thirty. Right on time. Guests would start arriving in the next thirty minutes, so Lydia needed to get on her way to pick up the guest of honor.

"Dang!" Vanessa exaggerated. "Y'all didn't get much decorating done." Neither Lydia nor Sandra commented. Between the three of them, they'd be done in no time with hanging the streamers, draping the table clothes, and placing the centerpieces. Lydia and Sandra exchanged knowing glances at each other, signaling that they'd continue their conversation later.

Lydia's mind was so preoccupied with her and Sandra's unfinished conversation that she didn't realize how soon she made it to the two-story townhouse in Southfield that Kania shared with her soon-to-be husband, Kenneth. Until they became serious about their wedding plans, Kania and Kenneth lived in separate apartments, not far from each other. The city of Southfield was located just outside the city of Detroit and was a thriving place for professional middle-class African Americans. Perfect for the attorney duo, Kania and Kenneth. Once they recovered from the cost of the wedding, they planned to purchase land in a subdivision near the same community.

There was no relationship among Lydia's friends that she admired more than Kania's and Kenneth's. She and Kania were like-minded when it came to the importance of independence and self-reliance of women. Kania was able to surrender to the call of love without compromising who she was as a woman.

Kania's place was immaculate as usual, her being the compulsive neat freak that she was. Everything was in its proper place. No magazines were sprawled across the coffee table but were neatly placed in the magazine rack. No pieces of mail all over the place, but neatly organized in a wall hanging letter rack in the kitchen. Whenever Lydia came over, she always left inspired to go home and clean up. Of course, she never did.

"Two more minutes," Kania called from upstairs, while Lydia was flipping through the latest *In Style* magazine, showcasing the hottest stars in their favorite winter fashions. No more than two and half minutes later, Kania came prancing down the stairs. Punctuality was another personality trait of Kania's that Lydia desired for herself.

Kania looked nothing less than fantastic. The usually conservatively dressed Kania, who always wore the basic browns, blacks, and navy blues, was boldly dressed in a cherry red spaghetti strap knee length dress, with a plunging back down to her tailbone. Lydia had never seen her look sexier.

"Girl, you look absolutely gorgeous!" Lydia complimented her genuinely, giving her the once-over as Kania turned in a circular motion allowing a complete view. "Kenneth's going to have to keep a close watch over you if that's how you're going to start dressing now that you're about to be a wife," Lydia teased, then added, "Hmm, he might have to start working with your firm, too."

"Chile, please. My man knows he doesn't have a thing to worry about. All of this belongs to him," Kania retorted candidly, running her hands along the length of her shapely body.

"Well, the party can't get started without you, so we better get going."

Inside the truck, Kania kept checking herself in the mirror. "I hope I don't look as nervous as I feel," she confessed openly.

Lydia glanced over at Kania's calm expression. "You're carrying your nervousness well. Besides this is only the bridal shower. You have a whole week before you can be rightfully nervous." Lydia flipped her left signal on just before merging onto the freeway.

"I wish I could wait 'til then. But as the days go by, I keep realizing that I'm getting closer and closer to pledging the rest of my life to Kenneth. As much as I love him, it still scares the hell out of me," Kania said honestly, resting her head on the headrest.

Lydia turned the music down. Looking closely at her friend's face, Lydia could see that she really was nervous. No matter how much two people love each other, the commitment of marriage was still one of the scariest things in the world. By far not an expert on love and commitment, Lydia was still compelled to say something to encourage Kania.

"You know, I've never known two people who are more perfect for each other than you and Kenneth. No union has ever been more right. I'm no Bible student, but I know there's something in there about a man finding a wife being a good thing, or something like that." Lydia constructed her words carefully. "You weren't one of the women out here on the hunt for a man. Kenneth found you, and he knew you were the woman God created just for him. Even though you put up a good fight in the beginning." She paused as a nostalgic expression crossed Kania's face. "You two are a match made in Heaven. As long as you keep God in your lives, you'll have a bond that no one can come between."

Kania squeezed Lydia's hand thankfully, a single tear falling from her mocha-shadowed eye. "I knew there was a reason you're my Maid of Honor."

"Yeah, yeah, yeah." Lydia needed to lighten the mood as they pulled into the parking lot of Vanessa's apartment complex. "No more tears tonight. This is your last weekend of fun before you turn into that traditional nagging wife, chasing behind your husband." The two friends shared a heartfelt laugh before making their entrance into the clubhouse.

NINETEEN

———※———

Kania's bridal shower was shaping up to be the success they'd imagined. All of the important and special people on the guest list were in attendance, and then some. Sandra was still barely speaking to Lydia. But Lydia went with Sandra's suggestion for the guests to wear nametags so that everyone could be on a first-name basis as they enjoyed the night's festivities. Lydia knew many of the people there. If there was anyone she didn't recognize, she properly introduced herself as any gracious hostess would have.

Everyone seemed to be having a good time, mingling with one another, expressing their happiness about Kania's big day the following weekend. Only one person seemed out of place. At first Lydia couldn't place it, but then it suddenly came to her. The face belonged to *Angelina*.

What was she doing here, Lydia wondered quite bewildered? Lydia waved her hand above the heads in Angelina's direction, trying to get her attention. If she was not mistaken, Angelina had looked right into Lydia's eyes, then turned in the other direction. No question, it was deliberate, which made absolutely no sense to Lydia. As friendly as Angelina had been the few times they'd seen each other at the health club and that time at the strip mall, why would she be standoffish now? Lydia rationalized that maybe whoever she'd come to the shower with had called her name or something and that's why she didn't acknowledge Lydia.

The scrumptious meal provided by a local restaurant consisted of seafood salad, baked chicken, green salad, and the softest dinner rolls Lydia had ever tasted. The guests were just as pleased. Lydia could tell by the way most of them kept a steady pace of fork-to-mouth.

Guests continued socializing with one another, laughing at the blushing bride to be as some of her law school friends and family shared funny stories about Kenneth's relentless pursuit of Kania and how he'd had to crack the whip to get her to marry him. Although Kania loved a good laugh, Lydia knew she would soon tire of the jokes being at her expense, so she suggested they bring dinner to a close and get to playing a few games, then to opening the gifts. An appreciative Kania secretly winked at Lydia.

The gifts brought on even more fun. One thing was for sure, Kania wouldn't be lacking for anything in the bedroom department. She received gifts across the board, including sheer nighties with matching robes, crotchless and edible panties, sex toys, and body oils and lotions. Lydia and Sandra couldn't believe that it was Kania's older relatives who had given the most sexual gifts. Her eldest aunt of sixty-seven years caused everybody's mouth to drop when she commented slyly, "There's nothing like good food and great sex to make a marriage last. Forget what those psychologists be talking about communication," she added, slapping five with another older guests.

"Going to bed angry makes for the best makeup sex," another one of the elder guests commented.

Lydia had been so busy helping with games, clean up, and gifts, she didn't realize that it had been quite some time since she'd seen Angelina. But quickly her attention was called to something else.

Kania was placing the last gift opened on the table when the music began. Recognizing the intro to sexy, R&B singer, Ginuwine's old song, "Pony", Kania gasped dramatically, immediately eyeing the obvious culprit—freaky Vanessa. "Girl, I know you didn't." But they all knew she did.

An entourage of sexy men with extraordinarily well-built bodies filed into the clubhouse, one by one, simultaneously gyrating towards random guests. While the guests were salivating over the entertainment, Lydia, Sandra, and Vanessa were quickly assembling the chairs for the show that was to come. After the dancers gave all of the guests a little excitement for the night, the main attraction made his grand entrance. He wore nothing but a towel and a black face mask revealing only his deep brown penetrating eyes.

"Kania Reynolds, front and center!" The man, who'd later become known as Hawk, demanded in a baritone voice.

Grinning from ear to ear while trying to be bashful, Kania rushed to the front to stand near the exotic, sensual man before her. The masked man glided Kania to a chair that was strategically placed in the center of the floor.

"These ladies are going to *wish* they were you by the time I'm done," Hawk promised as his music began to play.

Hawk definitely made due on his promise, at least as far as Lydia was concerned.

"Girl, I'm going to need to run to your apartment for a cold shower after that performance," she teased.

"Sure. Just hurry up so I can have the place to myself with Hawk." Vanessa laughed back.

It was nearing midnight when people began leaving. Most of those were relatives. Lydia noticed Angelina reappeared from nowhere right about the same time. Before leaving, everybody expressed what a great time they'd had and flocked around Hawk, gladly taking his business cards for private party bookings.

There were only about five women left in the clubhouse when Kenneth and a few of his friends showed up. As he'd had his bachelor party this same night, needless to say that he and his friends were still buzzed from the several rounds of drinks they'd had and weren't ready for the party to stop. But a lovesick Kenneth insisted on dropping in on his wife-to-be.

Within minutes, Kenneth and Kania were snuggled up together on a couch, and it was obvious that there would be no prying them apart. Vanessa, in a slightly tipsy state herself, suggested that, since there was still a good amount of food left, the guys stay there, and listen to music, eat, or play some adult games. The latter piqued the guys' interest, as was Vanessa's plan.

Exhausted, Lydia wasn't much in the mood for games. She agreed to stay on to help with the cleanup after she went to Vanessa's apartment to get Sandra, who'd retired there a short time ago for a quick nap before Lester was to pick her up. The last trimester of her pregnancy had caused fatigue to return, so Sandra had done good to have stayed this late. Besides, while Alicia was at her grandmother's house, the alone time would be good for Sandra and Lester, who was still trying to save his marriage.

After seeing Sandra and Lester off, Lydia headed back in the direction of the clubhouse. Though the area was well-lit, Lydia still quickened her steps, since crime was just as much a factor in the suburbs as it was in the city.

"What's your hurry?" A deep voice asked behind her. Lydia turned to see Roy, smiling.

Surprised and admittedly happy herself, Lydia smiled back. "What are you doing here, besides creeping up on women in the dark?"

He fell in step alongside her. "Hope I didn't scare you," he offered affectionately. "I was at Ken's bachelor party and decided to be his designated driver—you know, I'm not big on drinking. Anyway, I had to park the car in the back."

"Oh," was all she said as they reached the clubhouse door. There was much to be said between them, but they both knew this was not the time, so they joined everyone else inside.

Seeing that the guys had left a little food on the table, Lydia instinctively put together a plate for Roy. While she was walking over to Roy with the plate of food, she made for him, she caught a glimpse of Angelina again, this time, standing closely to Vanessa, engaged in a visibly personal conversation. That was even stranger than her being at the shower in the first place.

Did they know each other? Lydia couldn't help but wonder. She had no idea what they could be talking about, if they'd just met. They were clearly on the same page, their heads nodding in sync.
Vanessa suggested the first game. "Okay, okay everybody. We're going to play a game—Truth, Dare, or Promise to Repeat. Y'all remember how it goes," she added, laughing. Lydia thought it was pretty corny, but a few of the others seemed into it. But she waved them off, pointing to the mess that she needed to clean up.

"No, no, no. Don't even try it, girl," Vanessa chimed. "Everyone has to play." She pulled Lydia away from the kitchen, towards the guests. Vanessa instructed everyone to form a circle in a boy, girl, boy, girl pattern. Everyone complied. Ironically, Lydia and Roy were seated next to each other. Strangely, however, Angelina was seated across from Lydia and appeared to be glaring at her. In response, Lydia tried smiling, but only received a blank, menacing stare in her direction.

"What the hell is up with her? Lydia thought to herself. As soon as this silly game was over, she was going to corner Angelina if she had to and find out.

Everyone sat quietly while Vanessa explained the rules. None of them had played the game in years, but the rules didn't appear to have changed.

Since it was Kania's party, she chose who went first. She chose, of course, Kenneth. He spun the bottle that sat in the middle of the circle they'd all formed. The bottle stopped in front of Alonzo, one of Kenneth's groomsmen. He fell over laughing—for what, no one knew.

"Truth or dare," Kenneth recited in a boyish, playful manner.

Alonzo, a former college football player who still had that football player's stocky body build, wavered over his choices. Finally, he said, "Truth."

A sly grin crossed Kenneth's face. He eyed his other college friends before asking his question. Like they were in cahoots. "How old were you when you *really* lost your virginity?" Kenneth and his friends burst into laughter. Alonzo did, too.

"Aww, man, that's cold. Let me go back. Can I choose dare?" Alonzo asked, unable to keep from laughing.

"No!" Almost everyone responded in broken unison.

"Alright, man. Just wait 'til it's my turn." He covered his eyes before reluctantly revealing his answer. "Twenty-five."

"*Damn!*" one of the other guys said. "Wasn't that like last year?" His laughter ignited the same from everyone else.

Boastfully, Alonzo corrected him. "It was *two* years ago." More laughter erupted. Even Lydia couldn't contain herself. This game was turning out to be quite fun. Alonzo spun the bottle as the laughter died down. The bottle pointed to one of Kania's friends, Christian. Not many knew that Christian and Alonzo dated briefly after college. But his question was a dead giveaway.

"Truth or dare."

"Truth," Christian answered.

"What was the real reason you broke up with me?" *Ouch! Talk about a dangerous question*, Lydia thought. Maybe that's something they should discuss in private. Everyone was quiet, anxiously awaiting her response.

Smugly, she said. "Your performance in bed was weak as hell. But now I understand why," she laughed out loud, slapping five with her girl across the circle, while the guys cried out, "Aww, dawg. She dissed you!"

Then Kania interjected, "Now, Christian, that was not nice."

"Hey, baby, he's the fool who asked the question," Kenneth said of his own friend. "He's a big boy. He can take it."

"Yeah, I am a *big* boy," Alonzo buffed up, gesturing to his crotch. They all laughed.

The bottle spun a few more times, but never landed on Lydia. After the first two truths, the next few people chose dare. One guy was dared to sing and perform the legendary YMCA song. He complied quite theatrically, too. One lady had to do her best Beyonce "uh-oh" bootie dance. It was loads of laughter, to say the least.

Almost having gotten away without being chosen by anyone, strangely enough, Angelina called Lydia's name when it was her turn. Angelina looked more angry than ever. Although Lydia couldn't say that she knew Angelina very well, she was behaving very strangely tonight. She had no idea where this apparent attitude was coming from.

"Truth or dare."

Weighing her options carefully, Lydia chose truth. After all, regardless of what her problem was tonight, Angelina didn't know her well enough to ask her anything off the wall and embarrassing.

What a surprise Lydia was in for! Angelina's expression was hard and cold, sending nervous jitters up Lydia's spine while she awaited the question.

Slowly, but pointedly, Angelina scowled, "Why ...do...you...FUCK other women's husbands?" The question silenced everyone in the room. All eyes darted towards Lydia, bewildered, twisted, but inquisitive.

Surely she hadn't heard Angelina right. Judging from the mystified looks on everyone's face, especially Roy's, there was no mistake in what she had heard.

"*Excuse me?*" Lydia asked emphatically.

Angelina held her stance, daring Lydia to say something. She stood to her feet, planting her right hand on her hip. "I didn't stutter, you nasty little *bitch*! I've been waiting for just the right time to get at you." The verbal attack was just beginning.

The stares from everybody were burning a hole through Lydia. This was unbelievable! How could sweet, desperate-for-a friend Angelina have turned into this vicious monster in front of her. "What the hell are you talking about?'

"*Dang*, girl!" Vanessa jumped in. "You fucking that many people, you have to ask?"

"Shut up, Vanessa," Kania hissed. "Now, this is your friend. So you'd better get her ass under control," Kania warned. "Game is *definitely* over."

While everyone broke up the circle, still looking for what was going to happen next, Lydia began connecting the dots in her mind. The arrival of Thomas, the hang-up phone calls, Angelina's persistence at the gym, the brick through her window, and finally, the miraculous ending of the phone calls after she had told Angelina about the possible police involvement.

It all made perfect sense. Standing before her was Lena Daniels-Cunningham—Thomas' wife, confronting her in front of all of these people.

The circle began dispersing, most mumbling about the confrontation amongst themselves. Roy guided Lydia towards her belongings to get her away from the scene, but Lena wasn't finished with her yet. Lena grabbed her by the arm, pulling her forcibly away from Roy.

"You think you're going to just slip out of here with a different man on your arm, while you've been sleeping with my man for years?" Lena seethed, closing the gap between them.

Finally, Lydia had enough. Lena already put her business, in a twisted sort of fashion, out in the open. She manipulated her way into Lydia's life under false pretenses to do only God knows what after she was finished with her prank phone calls and vandalism. The longer Lydia remained silent, Lena was going to have the upper hand.

"Look, Angelina—oh, I'm sorry. I mean Lena. I'm going to deal with you like a *real* woman. It's clear what you think you know about what's been going on, but what you need to do is deal with your lying ass, cheating ass husband—like a real woman would!" Lydia was almost nose-to-nose with Lena

Lydia turned her back, going in the direction of her purse and jacket when, to everyone's surprise, Lena leaped on top of her. A few stood in awe as the two women tussled on the floor, throwing punches, and kicking at each other while Kenneth and Roy tried unsuccessfully to pull them apart. Lena didn't even back off when she heard Kania mention calling the police. Kenneth finally managed to get a hold of her and pull her and Lydia apart.

Hair disheveled, eye makeup smeared, Lena roughly smoothed out her clothes as best she could. "If I see or hear about you with Thomas again, phone calls and a broken window will be the least of your concerns. I know more about you than you realize *BITCH!*"

Lena left with no further words. But what else did she need to say after that threat? Lydia was speechless. She sat on the floor looking crazy, strands of her hair hanging out of the neat twist it was in when she arrived.

Unable to move, Lydia sat there feeling the stares of the remaining eyes, casting judgment on her with what they thought they knew. Roy came to help her, but she took the embarrassment of the moment out on him.

"I'm fine," she snapped. "I don't need your help."

"Umm-umm, girlfriend," Vanessa said loud enough to be heard by everyone. "You do need some help—help with your obvious problem of messing with other women's men," she added with a smirk, as she circled Lydia where she was standing, "See what happens when you mess with the wrong one."

"You set this whole thing up, didn't you?" Kania asked Vanessa angrily. "I can't believe you." Against Kenneth's protest, Kania approached her sister. "You'll do anything to mess things up for my special time. I knew you were jealous, but I didn't know you'd go this far to try to ruin my wedding. I don't even know what I was doing letting you have any part of my wedding!" she spat, filled with anger and disappointment.

Obviously, Vanessa had had too much to drink. Remorseless, she snapped. "*Fuck* your wedding! I didn't want to be a part of this *bullshit,* anyway. Mama is the only reason I'm participating at all.

Instead of being pissed at me, you ought to be directing your anger towards your whorish Maid of Honor," she spat indignantly. "She's the one who gets off on sleeping with other people's men, while trying to act all uppity and shit, like she's better than everybody else."

"*Whoever* Lydia is sleeping with is none of your business!" Kania shouted, trying to get Vanessa to see the bigger picture. "It wasn't your place to air anyone's dirty laundry, and certainly not the place to set up your little personal ambush. Next time you want to see a fight, do it on your own time."

"Umm-hmm, that's right," two remaining female guests agreed. As if just realizing that she had an audience, Vanessa turned brusquely to the door, but added before leaving.

"Party over! Everybody get the hell out of my clubhouse."

Lydia couldn't believe what had just happened. Everything bad that happened lately had a direct link to her involvement with Thomas. God, she was glad that was over.

Kania turned towards her, apologizing. "I am so sorry that Vanessa did this. I had no idea what she was up to when she asked me if she could invite a friend of hers."

"No, Kania. I should be apologizing to you. None of this would have happened if I hadn't started up with Thomas..."

Kania cut her short, shaking her head. "Nope. There's still no excuse for Vanessa's actions. If it wasn't this, believe me, she would have found another way to try to ruin this for me."

"I knew Vanessa didn't like me, but I had no idea it was this serious," Lydia said.

"And I had no idea you could hold your own like that," Kania said referring to the rumble. "At first I thought I was going to have to jump in and save you, but you got it together."

"I'm just mad that there wasn't any mud in the vicinity," Kenneth teased, pulling Kania close to him from behind. To Kania, he said, "We better get out of here before that crazy sister of yours calls the police saying we're trespassing or something." Lydia and Kania agreed.

"Is Roy driving you guys or me?" Lydia asked.

Kenneth glanced at her twisted. "Girl, Roy left about fifteen minutes ago. He didn't look too good either. I hope tonight wasn't the first he heard about all of this."

"Ken!" Kania pinched his arm.

"Hey," he began in defense of himself. "I'm just saying. I know how men react to things like that. All I'm saying is that you might want to let things blow over a minute, but talk to him as soon as possible, preferably after the wedding. I don't think we can handle anymore drama."

Kenneth was right. Lydia definitely needed to talk to Roy. It was unquestionable that his perception of her involvement with Thomas had just taken another turn for the worse. For sure he was thinking that she was knowingly seeing a married man. There was no way Lydia could let him continue thinking something as heinous as that.

Officer Boyle was standing at the clubhouse door when the three of them were getting ready to leave. This time he wasn't dressed in his official blues. From what could be seen beneath his three-quarter length brown leather coat he wore a pair of black loose-fitting Sean Jean jeans with some Timberland boots. Concern was clearly on his face when he saw Lydia.

He reached for her not like an officer would normally do for a victim, but like a man concerned about a woman. Even Kania and Kenneth were surprised.

"Are you okay?" Officer Boyle asked Lydia.

Lydia was taken aback. "Yeah," she said, motioning towards her face. "It looks worse than it feels."

"Where'd the perp' go?" Officer Boyle asked finally looking towards Kania, who obviously had made a personal call to her friend instead of 9-1-1.

"She got out of here when she heard me mention the police," Kania answered.

"Well I can get a hold of her address and pick her up," he began, but Lydia stopped him.

"Don't worry about it tonight. Let me sleep on it, think about how I want to handle this," Lydia said honestly.

She could tell he didn't like her idea, but he didn't push the issue. "I don't think you should be at your house alone, since this woman knows where you live. If she had enough nerve to pull this tonight in front of all these people, there's no telling what she'll do if you're by yourself."

Lydia continued protesting. "I really think the worst is over." It was obvious his concern was more than official, which was flattering, but at the same time awkward. The seriousness of the incident was becoming more real than Lydia wanted it to be.

"Ms. Love, this is not something you should take lightly. I'd feel much more comfortable if you agreed to my making some rounds around your house for a couple of hours. Nothing invasive or anything, just a safety precaution."

Kania gave her a, "please say yes" look. So she did, much to Officer Boyle's delight. He followed her first to drop Kania and Kenneth off at their townhouse, then to her own house.

On the drive home, being mindful of Officer Boyle's presence a couple of car lengths behind her, Lydia's thoughts were far from Lena

Daniels, and fully on how she was going to square things away for good with Thomas and salvage what, if anything, was left with Roy.

TWENTY

———— ✣ ————

Sleep was a stranger to Lydia as she spent the night tossing and turning shortly after arriving home from the disastrous bridal shower. A few times she checked outside her window to find Officer Boyle exactly where he'd been the last time she checked—in front of her house. He acknowledged her with a friendly wave. Shifting her eyes toward the digital clock, the time read two-oh-five, in the morning. It was useless trying to get some sleep. Her mind was too troubled with the mess she had created for herself. Pulling herself out of bed, Lydia put on her terrycloth robe and went downstairs to the kitchen.

It wasn't until now that Lydia realized how much she was behaving like the women she often criticized in magazines and on talk shows. The women who didn't know they had a good thing until they lost it. The women who couldn't let go of the men they know are no good for them until they finally hit rock bottom.

She rummaged through her cabinets for the Maxwell House instant coffee she always kept on hand for the rare occasion that she needed

165

a cup on a Saturday or Sunday morning. For the most part Lydia was a Monday through Friday coffee drinker. In the far back corner of the top shelf was the can she was looking for. What a relief! But that relief didn't last very long. There weren't even enough grains in the can for half a cup of coffee.

Now, Lydia had to figure out how she was going to get in her truck and get to the Tim Horton's only a few blocks from her house, without Officer Boyle getting on her case. Of course, she appreciated his concern for her safety, but he didn't run her. If she wanted a cup of coffee at almost three o'clock in the morning, she was going to get it.

Quickly, she pulled on some sweatpants and a sweatshirt. Since she was jumping right into her truck, she didn't bother with a coat. As she opened the door, Officer Boyle instantly got out of his car and walked purposely in her direction.

"Where are you going?" he asked, perplexed. After she told him, he was dumfounded. "Coffee! You can't be serious?" He tried to read her face.

"Look Offi...," she started, but he cut her off.

"Chris."

Smiling sheepishly, Lydia started again. "Ok, Chris. I really appreciate what you're doing. But if the woman hasn't come this way so far, she's probably not. I'm not going to be captive in my own home. I mean, what's done is done. It's over. I just want to get a cup of coffee."

"What if I get it for you?" Chris asked. "I can stay with you until the morning," he offered kindly.

Lydia's expression softened at the same time that her heart sank at his heartfelt innuendo. At a different time, and under different circumstances she would have gladly given more thought to his advances. As it stood, there was entirely too much going on in her life to even think about entertaining the possibility with the attractive, sweet-intentioned officer. Chris must have seen everything plainly on her face.

"I'll tell you what. You win. But at least let me follow you to your coffee spot." As he began walking towards his car, he added, sincerely. "Keep my number in case you ever want a man who can protect and then some."

After she watched Chris drive away while she was at the drive-thru speaker at Tim Horton's, she realized that she already had had exactly what he was offering. She had it in Roy.

The bright-eyed drive-thru attendant politely handed her the small French Vanilla cappuccino she'd ordered. Her bruised lip stung even more when the hot drink made contact. It gave her an instant reminder of Angel—Lena. Lydia realized that her anger wasn't as much as she expected toward Lena. After all, she never experienced one of her boyfriend's sleeping with another woman. At least, not to her knowledge. But she could only imagine how hurtful and devastating that must feel. It was only now that it made sense why Sandra was having a harder time letting this thing go between Lydia and Thomas. Even though she knew that dating married men wasn't Lydia's style, the reality of it probably reopened the fresh wounds of Lester's infidelity. Also, past experiences did indicate that Lydia had often acted out of character where Thomas was concerned.

Aimlessly driving, Lydia took small sips of her coffee with no regard to the stinging of her lip. No matter how hard she tried, though, her thoughts kept resting on Roy, and the embarrassment she caused him tonight, and the hurt she caused him from the moment she began pushing him away.

Roy had been everything Lydia needed in a man. In a friend. He was a man who held her when she needed to be held, made her laugh when her spirits needed lifting, and told her the truth about herself when she needed that, too. He didn't keep any part of himself off limits to her. He was always open about his heart's desire and his expectations.

He deserved better than what Lydia had given him. She only hoped that she hadn't ruined her chances of making things right between them. But she felt compelled to prepare herself for that possibility, especially after tonight.

Bringing her truck to a deliberate stop, Lydia shifted the gear into park. She wasn't sure at what point she began going in a different direction than her house, but she wasn't at all that surprised when she looked up to find that she was parked in front of Roy's house.

"What are you thinking?" Lydia questioned herself. Memories of the times she'd spent there came flooding back to her, along with thoughts of a future she had possibly ruined. She remembered the times he had made her breakfast after she'd spent the night or the Sunday mornings that they woke up together and took walks along the trail three blocks over. Tears filled her eyes, but she blinked them quickly away.

If she was going to face him, she needed to be strong. Tears would garner her no sympathy, she was sure. Roy would undoubtedly have questions he wanted and deserved answered or assumptions she'd have to clear up.

She tried, unsuccessfully, to muster up the strength to get out of the truck. Then she'd have to make her way to the door. As fear enveloped her, she realized she'd made a mistake. This wasn't the time. The news was too fresh. She needed to give Roy more time. *Maybe she'd already given him too much time already*, she thought conflictingly. But the truth was that it was she who needed more time, more time to prepare for the possibility of being rejected.

She had to get out of here. The decision was made too late. Roy's front door was opening. *"Oh shit!"* Lydia whispered, frantically. If she pulled off now, it would draw too much attention to her, being that she was only one of two vehicles parked on the street.

It was nearing three o'clock in the morning. Where he was going at this time anyway, she couldn't help wondering. Had he been watching her from his window? Maybe he had.

Or, maybe not, Lydia concluded, as the gut-wrenching feeling of a knife twisting in her stomach began. She'd been so caught up in herself that she didn't realize that Roy wasn't leaving his house. Quite to the contrary, someone else—a woman—was leaving. From the short distance Lydia was from the house, she recognized the woman's face. If Lydia wasn't mistaken, it was one of the guests from the bridal shower. Christian. Only then did Lydia notice the Wintergreen Honda Accord parked in front of her. The car must belong to Christian.

What the hell? Quickly, in hopes of avoiding being seen, Lydia slid down in her seat as far as she could go. Her breathing rapidly increased from the sudden anxiety attack she swore she was having. This could not be happening, but even through squinted eyes, the horridly embarrassing scene was playing out before her.

Please, God, don't let him see me, Lydia silently prayed to God. Still, though, as badly as she wanted to get away without being seen, she just as badly wanted to know what the hell Roy was doing with Christian in the first place. As far as she knew, the two of them hadn't known each other before tonight. And she hadn't even noticed them having that much contact during the short time Roy was at the clubhouse. "Damn, she moved fast," Lydia said maliciously of Christian.

Christian walked down the walkway, flirtatiously glancing back at Roy, who trailed a small distance behind her. Lydia cringed at the sight before her. Her body ran hot with seething jealousy as Christian peeled down the street.

All she needed now was for Roy to go back into his house so that she could get the *hell* out of there. The way her luck was running lately, that simply couldn't happen. Roy must have known she was there. Instead of going back in the direction of his house, he took long, purposeful strides toward where she was parked.

Roy appeared calm, controlled. It was apparent to both of them that he had the upper hand. When he reached the driver's side, he motioned with a nod of the head for her to roll down the window. Against her will, she complied. With the jagged edge of her once manicured fingernail broken during the fight, Lydia pressed the window control button as Roy stood looking on.

Unable to open her mouth to speak, she sat silently, first hoping and then not hoping he would say something, afraid of what that something may be. But after a silence that seemed forever, yet not long enough, Roy finally spoke.

"You should have called before coming by." His voice was emotionless, bordering cold.

Though he appeared relaxed, Lydia was still nervous. It wasn't a good thought or an appropriate one for the moment, but her mind was having a difficult time letting go of the vision of Christian bringing any form of comfort to Roy. Of course, she couldn't blame Roy if he had taken to the arms of another woman after what she'd been involved in with Thomas.

All she wanted to do right now was get home, back in her bed, to pretend this night never happened. Pretend that she never responded to Thomas' initial advances. Pretend that she never met his crazy ass wife! Unfortunately, there was no pretending this mess away. She'd have to deal with it, make it right—if she could.

"You're right. I'm sorry." There wasn't much else she could say. Her brown face was red with embarrassment. "I was about to leave when you and Christian came outside," she admitted uneasily. "I didn't want to be so noticeable leaving, so I was going to wait until you went back inside."

A knowing smirk crossed his lips. "So you really think you've been sitting in front of my house for almost ten minutes and I didn't know you were here? That might have worked if you had parked three or four houses down. I'm pretty observant, remember?"

Lydia was shrinking with embarrassment by the minute. "You're right. I'm going to go…"

"Do you want to come in? Or do I have to keep standing out here in the cold talking to you, while you're toasty in the truck?" Roy asked, surprising her. An invitation to go inside was the last thing she expected. For sure she thought he'd be telling her to go back to where she came from. She should have known Roy wouldn't be that cruel to her.

Then another vision of Roy making love to Christian crept into her thoughts. She couldn't shake it. As she prepared to decline his offer, Roy stopped her, speaking sternly.

"Look," he said pointedly. "Since I know you pretty well, Lydia, I know you didn't come here for no reason. Stop being so damned stubborn and come in the house," he demanded, leaving her little choice. Complying with his authoritative request, she followed him into his house, terrified of what was to come.

TWENTY ONE

Everything was just as Lydia remembered. Her eyes roamed the familiarity of Roy's house. She smiled, noticing that he still had all the trinkets she added when they were together, like the wall sconces, throw pillows, and the Annie Lee figurines she purchased off e-Bay. It was nice knowing that he thought enough of her to keep the personal touches that she added to his home, although he'd done a great job decorating on his own.

One of the first things she noticed on her first visit to Roy's house was that it wasn't decorated with meaningless pictures to look stylish. Instead, Roy had original, thought provoking art, which he could even engage in intellectual conversation about as well as explain their history and origin.

Roy had also come across as a neat freak, judging from his living room, dining area, and kitchen. But the real Roy was unmasked once you entered his bedroom, which was his personal domain, the place he really let go. Nothing meaningful or intellectual there. Just basic window coverings, black furniture centered perfectly in front of his fifty-inch flat screen television.

Nothing had changed, except that Lydia now felt like she was in a place where she no longer belonged. From the looks of things, Roy was moving on. Slowly, but nevertheless moving on. Eventually Lydia's things would be replaced with the taste and style of someone else, maybe Christian.

"Don't act like a stranger. Sit down," Roy directed her, after he returned from the kitchen carrying two glasses of water. He handed one to Lydia before sitting in a plush recliner across from her.

Roy was very handsome, Lydia noticed. As a matter of fact, he was even more handsome than the last time she'd seen him a few hours ago. Her heart sank, realizing it was probably the afterglow of sex that was making him so attractive to her. *That bitch Christian!* Lydia angrily thought, then immediately regretted it. She had no right to be jealous. But the feeling was too strong for her to deny. Christian didn't know anything about her and Roy's former relationship, not that it really mattered anyway. Roy was a single man, which made him fair game. Not everybody takes forever to decide what they want and then to go after it. Obviously, Christian was a woman who went for what she wanted.

"This was a mistake, Roy." Lydia said suddenly, setting her glass on the end table beside her. "I shouldn't have come here."

Roy's voice was calm in response, but the frustration was plain on his face. "Maybe you're right Lydia, but you're here now. And you came here for a reason."

She shook her head indecisively. Of course there was an underlying reason for her being here, but she wasn't quite sure how to put what she was feeling into words. Lydia never had to be the aggressor. She was used to men putting the moves on her. Fear of rejection prevented her from saying what she felt. Roy must have sensed her unwillingness.

"It's just me, Lydia. I'm still the same man I've always been. You're here because you have something to say. I want you to say it, no matter what it is," he encouraged her.

A few minutes passed before she conjured up the courage, with Roy's help, to open her mouth. "Okay, Roy. I'm not sure why I'm here. I got in my truck, going for coffee, for God's sake. I ended up here. I'm sorry I interrupted your uhm…uhm evening with Christian." She stood to leave again, then added contritely, "It's good to see you're moving on."

Roy stifled back laughter. "So you didn't have a problem seeing Christian leaving my house just now," he baited her.

Stuttering, Lydia returned, trying to hold on to what was left of her dignity, "I wouldn't quite say that. It was only a matter of time before some other woman came into the picture for you."

"Do you really expect me to believe that Lydia?"

"Believe what?"

"Believe that you're not mad as hell about Christian being here, number one. Number two, that you didn't intend to come over here. Can you be honest about anything anymore, Lydia?" he asked incredulously.

Indignantly, she retorted, "I've been honest with you."

Roy smacked his lips. "Oh, were you honest when you broke up with me to start seeing Thomas again? Were you honest when you told me that day at your mother's house that this thing with Thomas wasn't what I thought? Or better yet," he charged on, "were you even honest with yourself, your friends, and family while you were sneaking around with your married boyfriend?"

174

His attack was too much for her to bear. The truth of his words cut too deep. Her plan had been to tell Roy the truth about everything in her own time. He wasn't supposed to have found out like this. Lydia had been cast in the worst light. And she had no idea how to recover from it. No words formed in her throat. She made a quick dash toward the door trying to beat the tears that were about to gush from her eyes. Roy called behind her, taunting her.

"Fine, Lydia, go ahead and leave. That's what you do best, isn't it? Leave when it gets a little rough for you." Anger and frustration resided in his tone. "I'm not going to play games with you. I'll leave that for Thomas, since that seems to be his specialty and you seem to like it," he ferociously cut into her. "As much as I love you, I *will* let you walk out of that door. But as God is my witness, if you do, I won't be here if you decide to turn back," he threatened, though it had more of a promising tone. "So if you have anything to say, even if it's that you love Thomas, you better say it now."

Lydia froze mid-stride in his walkway. She looked back at him questioningly. "Of course I don't want to be with Thomas. I made that decision before I found out he was married. For weeks I've known that I don't want him. All I've been thinking about is what I want with you," she quietly confessed.

"Yeah, right," he spat harshly. "You're here because you're embarrassed about being confronted by the wife of the man you've been sleeping with. You're running back to me because it's where you feel safe!"

Frantically, Lydia rushed over to be face to face with Roy. "No! It's not like that." she cried. "Thomas has nothing to do with me being here. I'm here because I want to make you understand that I…"

She stopped short at the doubtful expression plastered across Roy's face. He wasn't buying anything she was saying. If only Roy hadn't been at that party tonight, she wouldn't have so much explaining to do. But the thought was useless, Lydia decided. Roy was *very* present at the party. And he had heard the simple truth about Lydia and Thomas from Lena's horrible attack.

Through his hard eyes, Lydia could still see the love he felt for her. But even the greatest love could be pushed to its limit.

"I can see there's nothing I can say to make you believe me, Roy, and I'm sorry for that. But I have to say this before I leave," she said quietly, before gulping the lump of fear that had lodged itself in her throat. "I love you. I don't want to lose you, and I'll regret it for the rest of my life if I have. I used to think the biggest mistake of my life was getting involved with Thomas. Now, I know the mistake was leaving you, and not recognizing the love between us as real."

She didn't know how she made it to her truck. Her legs were numb beneath the weight of her pain. In her bed later that night, the events of the night continued to replay in her dreams as she cried herself in and out of sleep. Flashes of Roy and the disheartening expression on his face crept into her mind, causing quite a restless night.

She had no one else to blame but herself for losing Roy. Not Thomas. Not Lena. Just her—the pitiful woman in the mirror. Now she'd have to live with the consequences of her foolish, and quite seemingly, irreparable actions.

TWENTY TWO

The next few days went by in a blur. Although Lydia slept through the entirety of the Sunday following the bridal shower, her eyes were still heavy when her alarm clock rang at six o'clock Monday morning. Trudging to the bathroom with laden feet, she took the longest, steamiest shower she could, hoping for some relief, yet coming up empty. After her shower, she searched her closet to locate her sharpest suit. Then she applied her favorite face powder, deep brown eye shadow, and sheer lip gloss. But in the end, despite her beautifully made up face, perfectly bobbed hair, and her best suit, she was still a pitiful sight as she glanced at her reflection in the mirror before leaving her house for work.

Arriving at work as inconspicuously as possible, Lydia avoided as much eye contact as possible. Somehow, she made it safely to her office, hoping she didn't appear as off-balance as she was. The last thing she wanted to do was alert inquisitive coworkers to the havoc going on in her personal life.

Lydia took careful sips of the hot cappuccino she'd purchased from a donut joint that she passed on the way to work. Waiting for her computer to finish booting up, Lydia flipped through the to-do list she made whenever she was going to be out of the office for more than a day so she'd be sure to remain on track upon her return. Luckily the only thing on her agenda was to catch up on her team's monthly observations, then write up yearly evaluations. That was enough to take her through the four days she planned to work this week, before the wedding. Unfortunately, there wasn't enough work in the world to keep her busy enough to keep her mind off Roy.

Thursday was her last day in the office, and the day was going just as planned, with the exception of a two-hour conference call with her peers in California. The call ended just before lunch. Since she'd been holed up in her office for the last few days, two of her peers, Veronica and Dominique, two of the office's most notorious gossips, convinced her to have lunch with them.

Over lunch, Lydia was brought up to speed on the goings-on in, and around, the office. Who was dating who? Whose marriage was falling apart? Who was pregnant? And so, on and so forth. Some of the things she heard even managed to put a smile on her face. But all of that changed when she reached into her purse to get her share of the bill and noticed her cell phone display flashing several dozen missed calls and two voice messages. Full of false hope, she scrolled the missed call log in search of Roy's number. Instead what she found was one call each from Sandra and her mother, and the rest, regrettably, belonged to Thomas' cell phone.

On the short walk back to the office, she checked the two messages on her phone. "Shit!" she cursed as she listened to her mother sound off about her bailing out of their scheduled brunch for the previous Sunday. Lydia was so torn up about Roy and what had happened at the bridal shower that brunch with her mother was the farthest thing from her mind. She made a mental note to call when she got back to her desk.

The message from Sandra stopped her in her tracks. She was half expecting some sort of verbal forgiveness or at least a suggestion for getting together. But it was better than she thought. Sandra's voice was groggy and soft-spoken. "Hey, girlfriend. I'm still mad at you, but not mad enough not to tell you about the birth of your new godchild. Besides I think you were paid back plenty to have been in your first fight ever in life," she stifled a laugh. "I went into labor early this morning. Come see us soon before they boot me out of here in, like, twenty-four hours."

Now, that was the most uplifting news ever! A new baby. And two weeks early. Lydia was ecstatic and couldn't wait until it was time for her to get off work. Thinking about seeing Sandra and the new baby had put the first sincere smile on her face all week.

The smile on her face was quite short-lived. In the time it'd taken for Lydia to go to lunch and get back in the office, something major had occurred. There was an awkward eeriness in the atmosphere when she and her two peers arrived on their floor. The warped expressions across the faces of those who weren't visibly trying to avoid eye contact were a dead giveaway. Lydia's first thought was that the announcement of the senior manager position had been made. If that were the case, however, the expressions wouldn't have been so dreadful.

"What's going on?" Lydia whispered out the corner of her mouth to Veronica, but she was clueless, too.

"One thing for sure, we'll find out soon enough." Veronica replied as they parted ways going to their separate desks.

Those who avoided looking directly at her, creeped her out more, Lydia decided, as she walked as normally as she could to her office when she really wanted to run for cover.

Finally in her office, Lydia felt safe from whatever the hell was going on. Eventually she'd be let in on whatever was going on, by someone in the "know." Well, sooner than she expected she would learn from a person who made a point to know everything going on in this office and others in the Global-Tel family. Marianne was sitting at her desk, not looking pleased at all. Actually, she looked quite perturbed.

Whatever news Marianne was going to deliver was definitely not going to be good. It was going to be very bad. Marianne was not a woman who showed her emotions so visibly. So for something to have made her so visibly distraught, it had to be monumental, to say the least. During the silence surrounding them, Lydia thought quickly what could have happened so terrible. Had someone died? *Ohmigod, Denise!* Lydia winced at the thought.

"It's not Denise, is it?" Lydia asked, praying that it wasn't.

Marianne finally spoke. Her voice was weighty. "That's the only good thing about what's going on," she began slowly. "At least no one's dead." Standing up from the chair, Marianne was dressed in a black pants suit and walked toward Lydia, still looking pitiful. "I just can't believe you messed up like this."

Lydia's head jerked in tremendous astonishment. "Messed up? Marianne, what are you talking about?" She was filled with concern and confusion. Marianne wouldn't even make eye contact with her.

A few minutes passed before Marianne spoke again. This was obviously difficult for her, but Lydia wished she'd just spit it out. The waiting was torture. One thing she knew was that this was more than the senior manager position being given to Angela or Stanley. Marianne wouldn't have been that distraught about it. It's not like there wouldn't be other opportunities for promotion.

"I'm talking about these!" Marianne shouted, flinging a few pages toward Lydia. "You really screwed up, girlfriend." Emphatically, she shook her head sorrowfully. "I only hope he was worth it."

The papers had fallen to the floor. Lydia stooped down, picking them up. Her eyes bulged in wild disbelief at what was before her. Snap shots of her and Thomas in very compromising positions in her bedroom, on her living room floor. Even one rendezvous that she had tried to forget about, in the back of her truck, had been captured on somebody's camera. Thomas had her so caught up in passion, she hadn't given one thought to being seen by anyone that day—yes, in broad daylight-- in the park. But, farthest from her mind was someone following them, with an obviously high-quality digital camera. The pictures were as clear and precise as could be.

Lydia's eyes scrolled to the top of the paper which bore the half dozen or so embarrassing pictures. Suddenly this bad dream had become a nightmare. Now Lydia clearly understood why Marianne's expression was wreaked with such despair. These pictures had been e-mailed to the entire e-mail distribution list of Global-Tel, including all levels of management. A simple message delivered a powerful punch:

I'm sure you don't want this adulterous, whorish woman representing your corporation.

It was signed, "Anonymous," but Lena's name was written all over. No doubt about that. Lydia was sure.

"This can't be happening," Lydia said aloud but more to herself, as her stomach plummeted.

"Well, it certainly is happening, baby girl. This is as real as real gets, Lydia, and it's not good. Whoever Ms. "Anonymous" is, she was certainly the wrong person to mess with. This *little* stunt of hers is resulting in HUGE ramifications for you." Marianne walked nervously around Lydia's office.

"I guess I really mucked up my chances for the promotion, huh?" Lydia asked, quietly.

Marianne's face twisted. "Mucking up the promotion is the least of your troubles, Lydia," she said in a tone more serious than Lydia had ever heard. It scared her, and with good cause, especially after what Marianne said next. "This is about the future of your employment with Global-Tel, Lydia. The powers that be want you out of here. This," she'd taken the papers from Lydia and waved them out towards her, "is totally unacceptable and grounds for termination."

"I'm being fired," Lydia screeched, truly not believing that this was happening. She began circling one spot on the floor, in a daze. How could so much go so wrong in such a short period of time, she wanted to know? *Fired?*

"As of right now you're to consider yourself suspended. Indefinitely." Marianne could barely get the words out. "You don't know how much I *hate* that this is happening. They wanted to have security waiting for you in your office when you got back from lunch to escort you out, but I talked them into letting me handle it. I figure that if anybody was going to walk you out the door, it should be me. I'm going to try to get this worked out in your favor. In the meantime, get this shit taken care of. And for good this time!"

Lydia wanted to say that the matter was already taken care of, that she was finished with Thomas before this travesty. But that was beside the point. Her job, her livelihood was in jeopardy. Her involvement with Thomas was on the brink of costing her two of the most important aspects of her life.

Through weighty silence, Marianne and Lydia packed the few personal effects that Lydia wanted to take with her—a silver framed picture of her and her mother together on their cruise, a picture of Alicia as a newborn, and an Annie Lee paper weight along with some other miscellaneous items.

It had taken only ten, fifteen minutes, tops, but it felt like so much more. Lydia felt like, or hoped, she was dreaming. She even closed her eyes for several seconds. Upon opening them, though, the box filled with her things was still on top of her desk waiting for her to pick them up and leave the building. And Marianne still looked as though this was one of the worst days of her life.

They embraced. Marianne cried. Lydia cried. Marianne told her to be prayerful. With the sentiments having been expressed, tears wiped away, Marianne told her to put on the strongest face she could muster up before they opened the door to walk through the office, for what Lydia prayed would not be the last time, with all eyes on her.

Without Marianne's help, Lydia absolutely would not have made it to her truck. After embracing one more time, Marianne went back into the building. Not even seconds later, Lydia broke down, and had the biggest cry of her life.

She cried for so many things. For her job being in jeopardy. For her relationship with Roy being in jeopardy. For her friendship with Sandra being shaken. For the embarrassment she suffered at the bridal shower and now this. She even cried for Lena's obvious pain—that she would go through such extremities to hurt Lydia.

Lydia cried for the entire ride to the hospital where Sandra was. A couple of times she had to pull to the side of the road to pull herself together. By the time she was directed to the maternity ward, to Sandra's room, Lydia had her poker face on, preparing to make real amends with her best friend and initiate a bond with her second godchild.

TWENTY THREE

❈

Lydia couldn't bring herself to tell anyone about the situation with her job. She only hoped that Ms. Lena was done with her humiliation tactics. A few times her thoughts drifted to Thomas, and whether he had any idea what his psycho wife had done. Only she didn't care enough to answer his incessant phone calls.

It was the weekend of Kania's wedding and Lydia planned to do her best not to get distracted by her personal drama. Turning her cell phone off was a positive step in keeping with that plan. All the important people, mainly her mother and Sandra, knew where she was. If anything pressing arose, they had the room number to the hotel and could reach her that way.

The wedding party was residing at the Marriott in the landmark Renaissance Center downtown for the weekend. Kenneth and his groomsmen would be in one room while Kania and her bridal party would be in another. The ceremony was to take place at a nearby church, where the reception would immediately follow back at the hotel, in the master ballroom.

This was the last night that Kania and Kenneth planned to see each other before becoming husband and wife. After the rehearsal dinner that night, the next day would be filled with hair and nail appointments for the bridal party, haircuts and grooming for the groomsmen. Then they would spend the last night as singles sleeping right across the hall from each other in joyful anticipation of the day, and most of all, the years to come.

Lydia thought she would have to try extra hard to put on a happy face for Kania this weekend, but surprisingly, it didn't take much effort at all. She was sincerely happy for her friend, despite the dreadful state of her own love life, and now professional life, too. That alone lifted her spirits, knowing that she could be so selfless.

Driving to the hotel by herself, Lydia took the time to finally return her mother's call from a couple of days ago, which would have been before her world really came crashing down. She needed some time in solitude to recover, so she stopped taking calls for the day.

Her mother's voice mail came on. Caroline and Deacon George greeted their callers with a scripture reading from the Bible—John 3:16, "For God so loved the world that He gave His only begotten son…" At the end of the greeting, Lydia apologized to her mother for not getting back with her and reminded her again of where she'd be for the weekend.

The ride to the hotel wasn't long, but it was long enough for Lydia to think back on her conversation with Sandra at the hospital. The nurse was taking the baby back to the nursery when Lydia entered the room. By this time, Sandra was looking ten times better than she sounded on the message she'd left for Lydia earlier that day. Her hair was wrapped and covered in a silk scarf. Her face was free of makeup, but still pretty au natural.

Lydia rushed to hug her friend. Instantly she felt a renewing of their friendship. She couldn't even get the apology out of her mouth before Sandra said, "No more apologies. It's a done deal. I must have been nuts to think that you'd be involved with Thomas knowing he was married. I know you better than that, even though you shouldn't have been seeing him at all."

The seat next to the bed that Lydia sat in was warm like someone had recently been sitting there. Sandra explained that Lester had taken a break to get something to eat in the cafeteria so she and Lydia could have some girl talk time.

"That's where we agree. I'm just sorry that I didn't tell you and Kania what was going on."

"Me too, but all of that is behind us now. What I care about is what you're going to do now with Roy. You've already let too much time go past dealing with this foolishness. You need to get him back," Sandra said encouragingly.

Sad and on the brink of tears for more than Roy, Lydia replayed the previous weekend's episode. "Needless to say, nothing's going to be happening with me and Roy, thanks to me," she added doubtfully.

Flippantly, Sandra talked over Lydia's bleak attitude. "Of course, he's going to give you a hard time after what you've done to him. But believe me, as much as Roy loves you, he's not going to let you go that easily. Just don't give up on him and do something stupid."

Sandra's encouraging words were at the forefront of her mind as she gave one of the hotel's front desk attendants her name and the party that she was with. She wanted to believe her friend's words, but Sandra hadn't seen the discouraging look on Roy's face.

A rosy-cheeked, rouged-lipped attendant advised Lydia of her room number and directed her towards the elevators. On the elevator ride up to the twelfth floor, Lydia pushed thoughts of her and Roy out of her mind.

"This weekend is about Kania and Kenneth," she reminded herself aloud before opening the door to join the other bridal party members inside their suite.

With a smile she greeted and was greeted by everyone. By five o'clock everyone had arrived except two of Kania's cousins who were in the bridal party. Kania was becoming frantic because the dinner was supposed to begin promptly at five-thirty.

"I knew I shouldn't have let their asses be in my wedding," Kania hissed in Lydia's ear.

Quickly placing a comforting hand on Kania's shoulder, Lydia reassured her. "It's okay, sweetie. Everything's going to be fine. It's only a quarter after. I'm sure they'll be here. Nothing's going to go wrong."

"Nothing?" Kania asked nervously, needing reassurance.

"Absolutely nothing," Lydia retorted confidently. Especially since her evil sister chose not to participate in the wedding after her antics at the bridal shower. Again, Vanessa thought she was messing things up for Kania's wedding, but little did she know, that Kania couldn't have been happier, since she didn't really want her there anyway. Kania's mother was the only one disappointed.

"Okay," Kania replied submissively. "I'm going to hold you to that."

Within an hour, everyone who was supposed to be present was, and everything was right with the world, at least as far as Kania was concerned. The wedding planner had things off and running at six o'clock sharp. And the woman must have been worth every penny she cost because she was definitely on point with the rehearsal and promised a repeat performance the day of the wedding. By the time she was finished with everyone, dinner was a much-welcomed treat.

There was so much love and excitement between Kania and Kenneth as they said their goodbyes to each other, that they almost had the entire wedding party, men included, in tears trying to pull them apart from each other.

When Lydia slept that night, she dreamed of Roy. They were enjoying a candlelit dinner. As soft music played around them, they were making plans for their own wedding. She was so much a part of the dream that she woke up almost in a panic when she didn't see the diamond engagement ring on her finger.

Time didn't allow for depression to set in. From the time they woke up, they were nonstop busy. While Kania had breakfast brought up from room service, she insisted the rest of the party indulge themselves in the full breakfast provided by the hotel restaurant, compliments of her and Kenneth.

After breakfast they spent the rest of the morning beautifying themselves for the big occasion that would take place in a few hours.

By two o'clock, the bridal party was ready. The bridesmaids were beautifully dressed in their silver, floor length, off the shoulder gowns. Lydia's dress, as Maid of Honor, was almost identical except that it was strapless. The groomsmen wore black tuxedos with silver vests.

The wedding chapel was nearly full by three-thirty. Following the strict instruction of the coordinator everyone was getting into place, just as they'd rehearsed, while Lydia calmed Kania's nerves and reminded her of how beautiful she looked.

"You are going to knock the socks off Kenneth when he sees you," Lydia assured her just before she herself was cued to walk down the aisle. Lydia's words proved true when she noticed Kenneth's smile broadening as Kania began walking down the aisle to the traditional "Bridal March" with her proud father.

The ceremony was a great success, and everybody was ready to let loose and have some fun at the reception. With the exception of having to pose for photographs periodically, the wedding party was having as much fun as the guests.

Lydia watched many couples, the newlyweds, and other couples, including Sandra and Lester, holding each other on the dance floor. She began daydreaming of what it would be like if she and Roy were holding each other like the other couples her eyes focused on. Leaning against the back wall of the ballroom, she closed her eyes, enjoying the reality of her daydream. She rocked to the smooth beat of the Luther Vandross love ballad being played, "Any Love," one of Lydia's favorites.

Then she felt the warm touch of a hand being placed on her shoulder. A touch she'd felt before. She didn't have to see him to know it was Roy. Simultaneously, she turned and threw her arms around his neck.

"Ohmigod, Roy. I knew you were here. I felt you," she said breathlessly, clinging to him.

But Roy's body stiffened. Gently, he pushed her back, creating a small space between them. It was then that she noticed that he was not dressed for the reception. Rather than a suit of any sort, he was dressed in blue jeans and a light blue polo-style shirt. She looked at him questioningly.

"I'm not here for the reason you think, Lydia. I'm sorry I had to come here like this, but it's your mother," Roy said, trying to talk over the music.

Lydia was confused, not sure she heard him correctly. "What?"

He grabbed her hand, pulling her into the lobby away from the music. "I said it's your mother. She's in the hospital..."

"Hospital! What the hell are you talking about? Why?" Lydia asked at once, hysterically.

Roy breathed heavily, straining over his choice of words. He took her hands into his. "You have to be calm, Lydia. Your mother was rushed to the hospital an hour ago. Deacon tried calling you, but your calls keep going straight to your voicemail. He called me because he knew I would be able to get to you. So I came to get you."

Lydia only heard pieces of what Roy said. All she knew was that her mother was in the hospital and she wasn't around when she had needed her.

Trying to be calm she snatched her hands from Roy. "Thanks for letting me know. What hospital is she at?"

"Henry Ford. But don't even think about driving yourself. I'll take you," Roy stated, matter-of-factly.

"No, thank you. You've done your duty. I can take myself to the hospital," she spat just as matter-of-factly. She had to find Kania and let her know what was going on. They hadn't gotten to the toasting part of the reception, so someone would have to fill in for her. Stinging tears in her eyes made it almost impossible for her to see anyone clearly.

Her search came to an abrupt stop when she bumped into Roy. "I'm not going to argue with you. I'm taking you to the hospital, no questions about it. I already told Kania what's going on. So let's go."

There was no fight in her. Right now, her mother was more important—certainly more important than fighting with Roy about how she'd go to the hospital. She glanced back briefly at the happy newlyweds headed to the dance floor for their first dance as husband and wife. At the same time that a tear dropped from her eye, she smiled at them. Silently, she wished them all the best. Depending on the news she received from the hospital about her mother, it could be the last time a smile would cross her lips.

TWENTY FOUR

The ride to the hospital was an emotion-filled one. Tension, anxiety, fear, and dread were amongst the emotions flowing through Lydia as she and Roy rode in silence. Of course, after the last encounter between them, the tension was even more magnified. Neither of them had the right words to say to the other, so silence was the optimal choice. Besides, Lydia was much more concerned about her mother and plagued with guilt over how preoccupied she'd been with her own life, so much that she hadn't spent any quality time with her mother in weeks. If anything happened to her mother…the thought was too distressing to complete.

Why is it taking so long? Lydia thought impatiently to herself. This is why she hated being in the passenger seat of someone's car, especially when she was in a hurry to be somewhere. It always seemed like the driver wasn't going fast enough.

Lydia couldn't help being fearful that the cancer her mother had five years ago had come out of remission. Since the last occurrence, Caroline had been taking fairly good care of herself, and visiting the doctor for regular checkups. She hadn't made Lydia aware of concerns lately.

As she prayed that cancer wasn't the culprit, she was glad to know that because of her and millions like her who support the American Cancer Foundation through regular donations and participation in yearly fundraising events that persons affected by the disease had even higher chance at survival. Still, she hoped her mother wouldn't have to go through that treatment process again.

Lydia sighed heavily as they finally reached the hospital. As if sensing what she needed, Roy took hold of her hand, squeezing it, showing a gesture of support before they got out of the car heading to the hospital emergency entrance.

The smell of sickness, heartache, and death rushed through Lydia's nostrils as they entered the hospital. Or maybe that was just her perception. She had hated hospitals ever since her mother's bout with cancer. Sometimes she still had nightmares about that ordeal. The thought alone of her mother being rediagnosed with cancer sent chills through Lydia's body. Again Roy sensed her discomfort and fear. Instinctively, he grabbed hold of her hand, squeezing it reassuringly as they walked in search of the doctor handling her mother's case. God, she was so grateful he was here with her.

Lydia's breathing had become erratic with nervous anticipation. Her heart felt as though it was going to jump clear out of her chest. *Calm down*, she urged herself. She would be no good to her mother if she had an anxiety attack and wound up in the bed next to her.

Only minutes had passed before they reached the information desk, but it felt closer to forever. Nurses and other medical staff buzzed all around her and Roy. Annoyance and impatience grew within her as she listened to Roy, unsuccessfully, try to get the attention of someone behind the desk. Then finally she heard a petite Asian lady respond kindly that the doctor would be out to speak with them in a few moments.

Roy continued squeezing Lydia's hand as they moved out of the way for others needing assistance from the medical staff. Not before long an older, salt and pepper haired man, who appeared to be in his late fifties or very early sixties, approached them just as they'd found two seats next to each other in the waiting area. Lydia tensed up again at the mention of her name.

"Ms. Lydia Love," the man who appeared to be the doctor in charge called out.

Quickly at attention, Lydia nearly leaped from the seat she'd barely gotten settled into. "Yes, doctor. I'm Lydia Love. How's my mother?"

The doctor introduced himself as Dr. Lewis and cleared his throat as he shuffled through a thick stack of papers held together by a faded brown clipboard. Nodding his head as he came upon the paper he had been searching for, Dr. Lewis made eye contact with Lydia, making her nervous.

"Ahh…," he began, but Lydia interrupted. "Is it cancer?"

He twisted his face. "Cancer? Uhhh…" He hesitated, shuffling through the papers again, which only frustrated Lydia more. "Oh, no Ms. Love. Your mother wasn't brought in for anything cancer related. No, she suffered a mild heart attack."

"Heart attack! Oh thank God", Lydia said. The words slipped out too quickly. She retracted them immediately. "I didn't mean it like that. It's just that I'm relieved to know it's not cancer. But you did say it was a *mild* heart attack, right? So she's going to be okay?"

"Well, your mother did have a clogged artery that could have caused much more damage than it did this time around. So she should definitely count herself as lucky. We just finished surgery clearing the artery. She'll be in recovery shortly and then you'll be able to see her. So, make yourself comfortable. It'll be a little more than an hour." Then he added, "Of course, she'll be a little groggy, but that's to be expected. Other than that, she'll be fine." Dr. Lewis left to tend to her mother with other medical staff.

Just as Dr. Lewis promised, Lydia was able to see her mother in a couple of hours. She had passed time falling in and out of sleep and drinking cup after cup of coffee brought to her by a very attentive Roy. But Lydia couldn't move fast enough to get to the room where her mother had been moved to.

Although Dr. Lewis warned her of her mother's groggy state, Lydia was still taken aback at the sight of her mother. Instantly, she thought back her mother's last hospital stay several years back. Those same twisty, unsightly tubes sticking out all over her body were just as frightening now as they had been then. Lydia gasped inwardly. Glancing at Roy by her side, she immediately felt comforted. Surely she would have fallen apart if he hadn't been there.

"I'm going to wait in the hall, okay," Roy suggested soothingly before exiting the room, leaving Lydia frozen in place at the entrance of the room. As badly as she wanted him to stay, she didn't have the nerve to ask him. He'd already gone over and beyond what she could have expected of him considering their current situation.

Walking as quietly as she could in the heels she had on, Lydia slowly moved closer to her mother's bedside. Caroline was so still and quiet. The only sounds were those of the machines monitoring her vitals and Deacon's breathing. Lydia sat in the empty seat beside Deacon George and moved closer to her mother.

Taking her mother's hand in hers, the tears began streaming down her face as the reality hit her that if God had so chosen, her mother could have been gone from this Earth instead of in a recovery room. She would have been so unprepared for that loss. There was still so much she needed her mother for.

Who would she have regular Sunday brunches with? Who would encourage her to stay in church? Who would know without a doubt if

Lydia were dating the wrong man? Who would be sitting in the front row of the church smiling proudly when Lydia finally got married? No one could take her mother's place.

This whole ordeal made Lydia realize how much she'd taken for granted the most important people in her life, namely her mother and Roy. She had already lost Roy. It would be hard as hell, but she could handle that. But losing her mother? That, she wouldn't be able to bear.

"It's alright, baby girl. God's not done with me down here," she heard Caroline speak weakly as she mustered the strength to squeeze Lydia's hand gently.

"Ma. I didn't mean to wake you," Lydia said, wiping tears from her eyes with her free hand. "I'm so sorry I wasn't here sooner," she began apologizing, unable to hold back the river of tears falling from her eyes. "I should have been with you."

A somber smile crossed Caroline's lips. "Stop all that crying, girl. Your being here wouldn't have stopped anything from happening. What's important is that you're here now. Besides, George was here with me," she continued. "That's what you need, honey. A man who loves you. A man who'll be with you when you need him. Stop wasting precious time on meaningless men," she added, both of them knowing who she was referring to.

By the time Lydia stopped crying and apologizing, she realized that Deacon George had slipped out of the room, and the nurse had entered to read her mother's vitals. Within a few minutes the nurse left them alone again.

"I think the doctor's going to release me in a couple of days," Caroline continued. "But you know George is supposed to be going to a convention with the pastor for a few days, and I really don't want him to miss it. Why don't you come spend some time with your mama while he's away?"

"Oh, Ma, of course," Lydia answered quickly. "There's no place I'd rather be. To tell you the truth, I was going to be there whether Deacon was in or out of town." They both laughed. The fact that she was suspended from work only made things easier because if not, she would've had to request some time off, whether or not it would've affected her chances for promotion. Clearly, that didn't matter now.

It wasn't long before Roy joined them. Lovingly, he hugged and kissed Caroline on the cheek. "You gave us all quite a scare, Mama. Better start taking better care of yourself, 'cause we can't handle things here without you, you know."

Caroline was smiling from ear to ear. "Hmph! Why do you think I'm still here? You can say that again. There's plenty of unfinished business I have to see to before I leave here."

"And what's that?" Lydia asked, finally joining the conversation. Purposely she looked past Roy's eyes, hoping her mother wouldn't sense the tension hanging between them.

"Never mind that. You'll know soon enough," she said before turning her attention back to Roy. "Thank you so much for being here, son. At least I know Lydia will always have you here for her when I'm gone."

"You guys will always be family to me—no matter what," he added, glancing at Lydia sideways, to which she shifted uncomfortably in her chair.

Shortly thereafter, the nurse came back to check on her mother, then told them that Caroline needed to rest. Lydia embraced her mother, wishing she didn't have to let go. But she did.

In the waiting room, Lydia and Roy exchanged pleasantries with Deacon George. He expressed his gratitude for Lydia agreeing to stay with her mother, explaining his wife was practically forcing him to keep his plans, which Lydia knew to be true.

After much debating, Lydia was okay with leaving the hospital for the night. Deacon George was staying overnight with her mother, and Lydia would be picking her up when they discharged her.

"I guess Kania can't be too mad at her Maid of Honor for ditching her at the reception because her mother's heart attack, huh?" Lydia asked Roy, attempting to break the awkward silence between them as they shared a corner table in the hospital cafeteria, drinking some rather strong coffee. A little cream and extra sugar made it better.

Shifting in his seat, Roy smiled, nodding his head. "Oh, I'm sure you did a well enough job fulfilling your duties to be excused for this minor emergency," he said jokingly.

Lydia laughed. It was good to finally laugh since she'd just spent the last few hours crying, worrying about her mother. It didn't hurt, either, for that laugh to be shared with Roy. Until this Thomas thing happened, she and Roy had shared many laughs together. And she missed them.

They spent a few more minutes talking around all of the issues between them—the wedding, her job, of course not the latest update, his job—but nothing about Thomas, his marriage, or their last conversation. When the small talk was complete the lingering silence between them returned.

"I meant what I said, Lydia," he said hesitantly, searching Lydia's eyes, "about always being there for your family."

"I know you did Roy," Lydia returned, starting to get up from the table, but Roy stopped her, grabbing hold of her arm. She sat back down looking at him quizzically.

"What I really meant was that I'd always be there for you, Lydia."

Stunned, Lydia remained silent for the first few seconds as she looked into Roy's dark brown eyes. Had she heard him correctly? Or was the magnitude of stress from all the recent events finally catching up to her. Saying nothing more, Roy simply held her gaze.

The cafeteria was filled with hospital staff, and friends and family of residing patients. But, at that moment it felt like only she and Roy were in the room.

"You don't have to think so hard, Lydia. You heard me right, and you know exactly what I mean. Just in case you don't, I'll explain." He took her hand in his and began stroking it gently with his fingers. "I was pissed the other night. It was my pride, my manhood, that was hurt more than anything. When you broke up with me, I knew it was something more going on than what you were telling me. I knew something was holding you back from me. And when I realized it was Thomas again, I figured you needed to realize for yourself who was best for you, and I was confident that you would realize it was me. I just didn't think it would take you this long.

"The thought that it took you finding out Thomas was married for you to come back to me drove me nuts. But then I decided to trust what you said. And I thought about how I felt the last few times we'd been together. I've never stopped thinking about you. I'm still in love with you, Lydia. When I saw you at the reception tonight, you looked so beautiful. I knew I couldn't be a fool and let you slip through my fingers. You know, just like I do, that we've been in the making a long time. Our time is here, Lydia. It's here."

Lydia was grateful that Roy was so full of words because she was so choked up on tears that she was completely speechless.

TWENTY FIVE

A janitor sweeping near Lydia and Roy's table interrupted the pleasant silence shared between them. When asked if it was okay to discard their nearly empty coffee cups, simultaneously, Lydia and Roy nodded their heads. Now that their silence had been broken, there seemed a need for someone to say something. Fortunately, as Lydia was still stunned by Roy's heartfelt words, Roy did the honors.

"Well," he said, standing up from his chair and ushering Lydia to do the same. "We have a lot to talk about. But there'll be plenty of time for that. We have your mother to take care of."

Lydia's heart skipped a beat. She liked the sound of that. *We*. For the first time, she was very comfortable being part of a unit. She was ready to embrace everything that came with it—good and bad.

"Besides," he continued, "you need to change out of that beautiful dress into something a little less eye-catching, even though you catch my eye in anything you wear." His expression was longing, sending shivers down Lydia's spine.

Lydia had almost forgotten that she was still in her gown from the wedding. She also remembered that she'd left her stuff at the hotel room since she'd rushed off with Roy to the hospital. But more than likely, she told herself, Kania would see to it that her things were dropped off at Sandra's place.

It was pitch black outside as she and Roy drove in the direction of Sandra's house. She hadn't realized how long they'd been at the hospital. It was close to two o'clock in the morning. Then it occurred to her to call Sandra to make sure she was even awake. Flipping her cell phone open, she had five missed calls. Sandra was sure to be one of them.

Just as she expected there were messages from Sandra and Kania, both sending their prayers and love for her mother. Sandra also said it was okay for Lydia to come by whenever she was ready to pick up her truck, that the keys would be in the mailbox if she was asleep. The other three messages were regrettably from Thomas. She didn't even bother listening to them. The sound of his voice disgusted her. Maybe he'd get the point of her not returning any of his calls and just leave her alone all together.

Sandra rushed to open the door when she saw Lydia approaching the walkway. It was obvious that Sandra had been up worrying about Lydia's mother's condition, too. She was just as relieved as Lydia was to learn that it wasn't cancer that her mother was dealing with. Sandra had been a monumental support for her throughout that ordeal. She couldn't have asked for a better best friend. No matter what either of them went through in their lives, good or bad, they were always there for each other.

Once Sandra was back in her house, Lydia walked over to the driver's side of Roy's car. Having shared a renewed closeness with him, she found it difficult to part ways, not to mention she didn't want him to be away from her and rethink everything he'd said to her.

He must have read her mind. Rolling down his window, he reached his hand out, touching her chin softly with his finger. "You don't have to worry about me. I haven't been the indecisive one. I know exactly what I want." He pulled her face close enough to his to plant a soft, lingering kiss on her lips.

Since neither of them wanted to be away from each the other, they agreed to meet at Lydia's house, and then ride to the hospital later that morning after they'd got some sleep. Roy started out of Sandra's driveway first. Just as Lydia was getting ready to pull off, Sandra called her back. Of course to be nosy.

Lydia knew her friend all too well. The closer she got to the front door, she started laughing as she heard Sandra singing in a whisper, *"Lydia and Roy, sittin' in a tree k-i-s-s-i-n-g, first come love, then come…"*

"And what's that all about?" Lydia asked innocently once she reached the porch.

Sandra wasn't buying it, though. "Don't even try it, girl," she said dramatically. "You know good and well I spied that lip lock between you and Roy."

Mockingly, Lydia repeated, "Lip lock?"

"Yes, lip lock—all over my driveway! So don't even try it. Just tell me you guys are back together so I can get back in here to this baby." Sandra stood boldly with her hands on her expanded hips.

Deciding not to keep her friend in dire suspense, she admitted, "It's nothing official. But you're right about him still loving me, despite the stupid things I've done lately."

"Thank God for that!" Sandra snuck in, before closing the door.

Lydia laughed all the way back to her truck. All jokes aside she knew that Sandra would be the happiest of everyone if things worked out between her and Roy. Not just because Roy was her cousin and Lydia was her best friend, but also because she'd get the credit for finally being a successful matchmaker.

Checking the clock on the dashboard, Lydia realized that Roy had a good ten minutes of driving time ahead of her. She and Sandra didn't stay that far from each other, so Roy would probably get to her house before she did. Lydia pressed harder on the gas pedal, increasing her speed enough to make better time.

Eight minutes later, she was pulling into her driveway. Her heart sank when she saw that Roy's car wasn't there. Maybe he changed his mind, she thought disappointingly. *"Dammit!"* She knew she didn't deserve such a perfect ending.

Sluggishly, she climbed out of her truck and headed inside her house, while she continued to wonder what happened to Roy. Could he really have had a change of heart in such a short time period? It wasn't like him to do something like ditch her, even if he did have second thoughts. He would have at least made sure she made it home safely first.

Oh, God, what if he had an accident or something, she thought, horridly? Immediately she rushed to the phone in the kitchen and dialed his cell phone. By the second ring, she breathed a sigh of relief when he answered. *Thank God*, she said to herself.

"Where are you? I thought you would have beaten me here," she asked calmly, glad he was all right. Roy explained that he stopped for gas since he saw her talking to Sandra.

"I'm just a few minutes away."

A smile big enough to fill the entirety of her house crossed her face. She didn't rush to conclusions, but she knew that with Roy spending the night, they just might consummate their reunion with

203

sweet lovemaking. She wanted to be ready when he got there. Quickly, she dashed to her bedroom, slid out of her dress, and jumped in the shower. Two minutes later she was dousing her body with her favorite cucumber-scented body spray.

Lydia was admiring herself in the purple lace camisole and matching lace French cut panties when she heard a knock on the door. Punctual as usual, she thought, traipsing down the stairs to greet Roy with open arms. Only it wasn't Roy at the door. It was a very grim-faced Thomas.

"What the hell are you doing here?" Lydia scowled, closing the robe she'd put on before coming down?

Thomas roughly pushed his way past her into the house. "I guess you weren't expecting me."

Ignoring him she asked again, "I said what are you doing here?" Lydia hadn't had time enough to prepare all the things she wanted to say to him. This was hardly the time anyway. He had no right to appear at her home just because he felt like it!

"I knew your ass was up to something. All you've been doing over the past two weeks is avoiding me, playing me like a fool." He began pacing the floor of her living room. "And I almost believed that shit about you being busy with your friend's wedding this weekend. Now I see the truth with my own eyes," he growled, looking her menacingly up and down.

What nerve! She fumed to herself. "Thomas, I didn't lie to you about anything. I was doing exactly what I said I was."

"Yeah, only you conveniently left out the part about hooking up with your letter writing ex-boyfriend, you lying little BITCH!" Suddenly close up on her, Thomas grabbed hold of her arms tightly. "Did you think you could keep hiding this from me? I'm not stupid. I've been watching you all weekend," he said shaking her angrily. "I saw your *punk-ass* boyfriend pick you up from that hotel. And I know that's who you thought was at your door."

"Let go of me!" She tried to force him away, but his strength was too much for her. "What I do is none of your business," she managed to say as she struggled to free herself from his mighty grip. "The only woman's business you need to worry about is your *wife's,*" Lydia spat, finally freeing herself.

Shock registered across his face. Perspiration had already begun forming along his brow as anger surged through him. Then a smirk crossed his lips. "Yeah, speaking of my wife, now she's threatening to leave me and using those damn pictures she has of us to make sure I can't get any form of custody of my son."

"Sounds like a personal problem to me," Lydia said, smirking. "Maybe you should have thought about that before you started cheating on her," Lydia said.

"You think this is some kind of *fucking* joke," he said, slapping her so hard across her face that she fell backward against the wall. The crazed look in his eyes frightened her. Thomas looked angry enough to really hurt her. She'd never seen him like this.

"Where's your smart mouth now, huh?" His breathing had become hard and erratic. His eyes darted back and forth as he was contemplating his next move. Lydia remained frozen where she fell, rubbing her stinging cheek, too afraid to move.

Daringly, she managed to say, "It's not my fault she wants to leave you. I didn't even know about her."

Thomas was pacing back and forth. "This is not the way it's supposed to happen. I was going to leave her after I got things straight with you. Now you're *FUCKING* all of that up!" He lunged for her again. At the same time the phone started ringing. Quickly she leaped from the spot where she sat, making a dash for the phone that was on the dining room table. *Maybe it's Roy,* she thought frantically. She almost had the phone when Thomas grabbed the hem of her robe, causing her to trip and fall. A stifled moan escaped her lips as she and the phone went crashing to the floor. "Ooww!"

Suddenly, she heard a noise coming from her front door, catching her and Thomas' attention. The door flew open. Roy came charging in.

"What the hell…?" Roy shrieked when he saw Thomas tugging at Lydia's leg. Swiftly, he ran in their direction, knocking Thomas in the opposite direction. Lydia immediately scrambled out of the way of the ensuing brawl. She watched in horror as Thomas and Roy threw vicious swings at each other, trying to tear each other's heads off. Frantically, she dialed 9-1-1 as she looked on in frightening despair.

TWENTY SIX

L ydia never believed that things could have escalated to this level. She once counted herself as lucky to have made it this far into her life without being assaulted by anyone, let alone someone she had once cared so much for. That is until now. She never thought she would have been among the many women who had so misjudged a man.

Never in a million years did she ever think that Thomas was capable of trying to hurt her. Certainly not physically. He'd already done enough to her emotionally. Thomas had only himself to blame for his predicament with his wife, or soon to be ex-wife. It was his own lying and deceitfulness that caused his problems.

Ironically, Officer Chris Boyle was one of the two officers dispatched to her house from the 9-1-1 call she made. Lydia watched Chris and the other officer struggle to get a very resistant, out of control Thomas into the backseat of the squad car. She shuddered to think of what Thomas would have done to her had Roy not shown up when he did.

Chris walked over to her to take her statement while the other officer kept watch over Thomas. Step by step, Lydia explained what happened. Chris was professional throughout the process, but his attraction to Lydia was still very evident.

As soon as Chris got into the squad car and pulled off, Roy came up behind her, pulling her in close to his chest, wrapping her in his arms. A feeling of safety and security enveloped her. It was at that moment that she knew Roy really would always be there for her.

"I always knew you were sexy as hell, but with all these men trying to get at you like this," he said, alluding to Chris, "I'm going to have to take up boxing."

A small laugh slipped from her lips, but seconds later Lydia was overcome with a rush of all the emotions that had built up within her over the past several hours. Before she knew what hit her, she let out a loud cry and turned into the comfort of Roy's strong embrace. She cried silently outside, trembling under the silhouette of the moonlight, until Roy led her into the house.

An hour passed. Lydia didn't know it, but she and Roy had fallen asleep on the couch, and she was lying atop his chest. The clock on the mantel read four forty-five. Having fallen asleep many times on her couch, she knew they'd both regret it in the morning, so she began shaking Roy gently. Once his eyes opened and she was sure he was awake, she said, "Let's go upstairs."

The short distance from the living room to the bedroom was filled with sweet memories of the many nights that she and Roy had walked this very path. It had been months since they'd been together, but it felt like years. Looking at him, she could tell he was having similar thoughts.

Lydia should have been embarrassed at the unsightliness of her room. Her bed was unmade, clothes strewn all over it and the floor from packing. It was good, though, that she didn't have to put on airs with Roy. He accepted her as she was.

The two remained silent as Roy began undressing. Too bad Thomas had ruined any chances of her and Roy sharing any romantic time together, Lydia thought. Not only was it too late, but she also noticed Roy wincing from a bruise that was forming on his bottom lip where Thomas landed a good punch. Romance was probably the last thing on his mind.

Seeing him comfortably in her bed, Lydia headed to the bathroom for some peroxide, cotton balls, and two Motrin tablets. It was the least she could do for the man who'd done so much for her in the course of twenty-four hours—supporting her at the hospital with her mother, welcoming her back into his life, and saving her from a maniacal ex-boyfriend.

Roy had begun nodding off when she reentered the room. "Hey," she said softly, rubbing his bare shoulder. He stirred at her touch. "I need to rub some of this on your…" Her sentence went unfinished as Roy pulled her on top of his body.

"The only thing I want you to rub on me is you," he said huskily, planting a wet kiss on her lips. Neither of them gave any thought to the cut on his lip as they wrapped their lips around each other's. The kiss was long, deep, and filled with longing passion that had been hiding within them over the past several months they'd spent apart from each other.

Staring deep into each other's eyes, they finally came up for air. Lydia had long since dropped the cotton balls and peroxide to the floor. Right now, all she wanted was this man in front of her—this man who'd loved her despite her mistakes.

"God only knows how much I love you, Roy," she said breathlessly. Pulling the covers down to expose his lean but muscular body, Lydia straddled him as he continued to look almost through her. "What's wrong?"

His eyes pierced her soul deeply. "I could never believe anything more than I believe that. That's all I've ever wanted to hear you say." Roy pulled her gently by the crook of her neck so that they were almost nose to nose. He began placing soft wet kisses along her forehead, the tip of her nose, then down the length of her neck. Lydia's eyes remained closed as she basked in the sweetness of him. She didn't open her eyes until she felt him pull away.

Wondering what had taken his attention away, Lydia sat at attention. When she did, his eyes were there to capture and hold her gaze. His eyes were dark and penetrating. She wanted to speak, but no suitable words would come.

"What is it Roy?"

An expression of sincerity crossed his face. "I love you so much, Lydia. I've known it since the first day I met you." She smiled as he continued pouring out his feelings. "The more I got to know you, I knew that I wanted to spend the rest of my life with you. Even when you kept pushing me away, I knew we'd be together."

He paused as he stuck his hand under the pillow. Lydia breathed in deeply when she saw the small jewelry box in his hand when he pulled it from under the pillow. "Ohmigod, Roy," she whispered. But he quieted her, pressing his finger against her lips.

"It's no surprise what's in this box, I'm sure. I've asked you to marry me before, but I never presented you with a ring. That's because, deep down, I knew you weren't ready. I was just preparing both of us for this moment. I bought this for you the day after you showed up unannounced at my house last weekend," he said, opening the box.

A sparkling, one-karat princess cut diamond ring was inside. Roy removed the ring slowly from the box while tears streamed from

Lydia's eyes. This was like a dream. But reality set in when she felt the ring slide onto her finger.

"Lydia Love, you are the love of my life. I will do anything for you. And it would be *my* honor to be your husband. Will you marry me?"

Between sobs, Lydia managed to muster a tearful acceptance to Roy's proposal. They spent the rest of the morning practicing how they would make love to each other every morning when they became husband and wife.

Two months passed. Lydia had wanted to put the entire Thomas and Lena ordeal behind her. But Officer Boyle refused to let Lydia out of pressing charges.

"Lydia, you've been victimized twice now. The only way to not continue being a victim, especially to the same people, is to send the message that you take it very seriously. Maybe sharing this type of bond will bring Mr. and Mrs. Thomas Cunningham closer together and they can move on with their lives together. Of course, along with a restraining order to stay away from you." After talking it over with Roy, Lydia opted not to press charges, but to file for the Personal Protection Order against both Thomas and Lena. After she came back from the station, Roy teased her, saying that Officer Boyle was just looking for an excuse to see her again.

Lydia was just glad that Thomas had never tried to contact her after he was arrested. Never in her worst nightmare did she think such drastic events would have to occur for the ties between her and Thomas to finally be broken. But she was glad for it. She and Thomas were finally a permanent thing of the past. When she walked out of the police station, Thomas and his wife were behind her. And she wasn't looking back. She was much more concerned with the future that she and Roy were planning together.

Vanessa, Kania's sister, even mustered up the courage to apologize for instigating Lena's harassment against Lydia. Apparently, Vanessa knew Lena from high school. Through Kania's and Lydia's friendship, Vanessa knew all about Thomas and Lydia's relationship. She put two and two together, figured that Thomas was seeing Lydia on the side when they moved back to Michigan, and encouraged Lena to get into the mix of things. It was over now. Lydia saw no point in holding grudges, though she knew that she and Vanessa would never be friends.

Soon after her mother recovered from the heart attack, Lydia and Roy almost gave her another one when they announced their engagement. Lydia would have been content eloping, but neither Caroline nor Roy would entertain such a thought. It had taken too long for them to get together for them not to celebrate with the big, beautiful ceremony they both deserved. Plus, Sandra would not allow another wedding to happen with one of her friends where she couldn't be in the wedding party.

Sandra and Kania couldn't wait to get Lydia to themselves for their ladies' night out to celebrate the joyous occasion. Along with Lydia's surprise engagement, there was even more to celebrate. Sandra had finally convinced Lester to seek counseling for his adulterous ways. It was the only way she would agree not to divorce him. Lydia and Kania gave their support to Sandra and wished her and Lester the best.

Even more surprising was Kania's announcement that she was pregnant. Everybody assumed that she and Kenneth, being so career-oriented, would put off having children for awhile. Obviously, they were wrong!

So there was a lot to celebrate between them. Lydia invited her girls over on Sunday morning for a home- cooked breakfast. Not only because she hadn't cooked for them in awhile, but more so to make up for not treating them like the best friends they were to her. While they both assured her that there was no making up to do, Lydia insisted.

"Just don't let it happen again," Kania said.

"Not that we have to worry about that anyway," Sandra added.

As she served them fluffy buttermilk pancakes, cheesy eggs, and sausage links, Lydia confided in them the full details about what happened at her job. As far as everyone knew, Lydia had taken some approved stress days off after everything that happened with the Thomas' attack on her. Sandra and Kania were speechless when they heard the truth.

"That little hussy!" Kania broke out. "She needs a back alley beat down."

Sandra was more solemn. "You almost lost your job over this mess? Did you tell Roy about that part?"

Lydia joined them at the table. "Definitely. No way I was going to keep him in the dark about anything else. We both agreed that keeping my job far outweighs my not getting the promotion. Other opportunities will come along. Marianne really went to bat for me, getting my discipline knocked down to a two-week suspension. I'll be forever grateful to that woman."

"How do you walk around that office with everybody having seen those pictures?" Kania wanted to know.

"Not much else I can do except keep my head held up high and thank God that I always work out. 'Cause a sistah's body was at least tight!" Lydia joked.

"Girl, you are a mess!" Sandra said, laughing.

"You know ain't nothing going to change about that." Lydia said as the three of them enjoyed the laugh together. One other thing that wouldn't change would be the bond of their friendship getting them through everything they encountered.

The End

Made in the USA
Columbia, SC
20 May 2021